Virginia Reels

ILLINOIS SHORT FICTION

VIRGINIA REELS

Stories by
William Hoffman

UNIVERSITY OF ILLINOIS PRESS

Urbana Chicago London

This project is supported by a grant from the National
Endowment for the Arts in Washington, D.C., a Federal agency.

"The Spirit in Me," "The Darkened Room," and "Amazing Grace"
were first published in the *Sewanee Review* 82 (1974), 83 (1975),
and 85 (1977). Copyright 1974, 1975, 1977 by the University of
the South. Reprinted by permission of the editor.

"Sea Tides," *McCall's,* September, 1966.
"Your Hand, Your Hand," *Carleton Miscellany,* Fall/Winter, 1971/72.
"A Darkness on the Mountain," *Cosmopolitan,* February, 1969.
"A Southern Sojourn," *Transatlantic Review* no. 49 (Summer, 1974).
"A Walk by the River," originally entitled "The Gorge," *Sewanee
   Review* 86 (Summer, 1978).
"Sea Treader," *Saturday Evening Post,* Fall, 1971.

Library of Congress Cataloging in Publication Data
Hoffman, William, 1925-
   Virginia reels.

   (Illinois short fiction)
   CONTENTS: The spirit in me.—Sea tides.—The darkened
room.—Your hand, your hand.—Amazing grace. [etc.]
   I. Title.
PZ4.H699   Vi   [PS3558.03464]   813'.5'4   78-16613
ISBN 0-252-00702-6
ISBN 0-252-00703-4 pbk.

For
Henry William Hoffman
hero, long term

Contents

The Spirit in Me

I look across pale corn to the dusty road between wooded mountains and see the dust itself rising behind the blue car moving too fast. She, the lady of the manor, comes again in early summer when heat of city rasps her flesh and her flatlands turn hard and red brown like dried blood.

She comes from Virginia west to ancestral acres, a jagged country of rock outcroppings and mountains gutted and scarred. She rests in deep shade at the mansion her great-grandfather built, three stories of dungeonlike stone topped by a copper roof which glints in noon sun. She comes with sin.

Her blue car passes my church, a board-and-batten building hammered together by my father, the roughness of new lumber first against his hands and then against my own. As a boy I labor with him evenings, carrying buckets of water from the stream which wrinkles over mossy rocks. I hoe the mortar, my blade furrowing the gray. As a young man I hammer on the new roof after a north wind curls off the old tin. In the beginning there are brethren to help.

"She's back," they say each summer. "She's returned."

"Cast your eyes down," I say.

"She lets us fish in her lake," LeRoy Ackers says. He is an electrician at the mine. I've seen him with sparks falling around him like a fiery rain.

"In Beelzebub's pond," I say.

She wears green, yellow, and lavender, her summer dresses bright around pampered flesh of her neck and arms. She has green, yellow, and lavender shoes, and perhaps underneath she wears those colors too, if she wears anything at all.

When she drives into our dusty town, she passes the granite court-house and iron cannon splotched by pigeons. Men stand on narrow buckled sidewalks which are mountain shaded, their bodies stilled, the skin taut across their faces. They watch the brace of her shoul-ders and the swing of her silken calves as she walks into the stone post office. They breathe the air after her, their nostrils searching out her perfume.

"She lets us hunt her woods," Perry Henry says. Perry's sharp bulldozer blade carves chunks from the mountains.

"She is the huntress," I say.

As a boy, before I become an instrument, I watch her. I climb from the cabin in my father's hollow, the cabin held level on the mountainside by smooth flat rocks hauled from the creek. I hide in sycamores to look over the stone wall beyond which she and her girl-friends play croquet on the grass. Her black hair is tied with a white ribbon.

A black man catches me up the sycamore. His name is Darce. He circles the tree and yells, but I don't move. I lie wound about a limb, my face down into leaves.

"I'll get me an ax!" he threatens.

The girls, holding their striped mallets, stand watching, and the mother, a fair woman wearing a white sunhat, hurries from the mansion, her fingers pinching up the white dress in front of her thighs. The girls point at me and laugh—only not the girl, who speaks for me.

"He's not hurting anything," she says.

"But he shouldn't be up there," the mother says.

"It isn't wrong to climb a tree, is it?" the girl asks.

I believe then she knows me as I know her, that she's seen me in town when she's driven through by Darce. I am already dreaming, dreams in which there are dirtiness and blood. She floats up from flowers of her mother's garden, from among the yellow blooms, her skirt belled. I fall on grass among the croquet wickets. She leaps and drifts down on me, the black heels of her shoes lighting on my chest, sinking red into my chest, while she smiles, until I am covered by her perfumed and gently lowering skirt.

Then in me pumping begins, the terrible pumping. I wake soiled and afraid. The night around me, I wash in the cold creek.

I believe she must cause my dreams. I stand on the sidewalk waiting for her to pass. An afternoon she sits in the car while her mother mails packages at the post office. I walk close, but the girl goes on talking to Darce, who waits to open the car door for the mother.

"What you staring at, big-feet?" Darce asks me.

"Who is it?" the girl asks.

"The boy with big feet who was up the tree," Darce says.

"Oh," she says and only glances at me. "I thought he had red hair."

I walk away, climb the side of the mountain, and roll rocks down, watching them smash through laurel and bounce across the black highway. I almost hit a silver gasoline truck. The driver gets out and shouts curses up the mountain. I hate her but I still have dreams.

"They was common once!" my father rages when they arrest him because of snakes. "The old man didn't have a pisspot when he first come to these mountains. My grandfather fed him. He'd have starved the winter withouten my grandfather's hog and hominy!"

I am afraid of dreams and the stains on myself. No water washes me clean. That summer I go into the mountain, into the wet blackness of the mine which has the sulphuric smell of the pit. The first days as I work setting locust props to hold the roof, a blue light flashes before me and cracks like a thousand whips. All the hair is singed from my body. I am thrown on the haulway floor among gobbets of coal. The whips crack through the mine, and a voice says, "You are my instrument!"

My eyes ablaze with thunderbolts, I am carried from the mountain and laid on cinders where I am born again. The sun in my face is not as searing as the flame I've seen. Fire damp they call it—methane—but I know Whose terrible power has rent the darkness.

"Glory!" my mother says, already dying, already shrunk so her toadstool skin drapes her bones like cloth worn thin. When she coughs, part of her insides come up and are spat on the ground.

"I heard the whirlwind," I say.

"O glory!" she says. "You done blessed this house like your father."

My father has died in a roof fall and lies on the mountain among crooked tombstones and purple thistle. My mother and I go to our knees. We hold each other and sway against the patched quilt on the bed.

"Take my boy and use him!" she calls. She is crying.

I dream no more.

During winters they keep Darce and his black wife at the manor above the town. In summer green comes to cover earth scars, and the mansion is so planted with trees and shrubs that only the copper roof and part of the wall show, but winters the earth opens its sores, and the wind shrills off the mountain like icy Hellhounds. The mansion stands alone in the wind, the stones like a tomb over us. No crow or hawk dares fly into the blast.

"It was built on our blood," the union man says. "Every lump of coal hauled out has our blood on it."

"Yet they send baskets at Christmas," my sister Renna says. She is a thin lorn woman who plays a golden cornet for the Salvation Army.

"Food spiced with brimstone," I say.

I am a man, and the girl becomes the lady who, like her mother, returns in summers, after a time with a husband, an army officer who brings horses on a railroad car and rides the ridges, he in brown boots and a campaign hat, cantering along the trails left by timbering crews, among stumps, hoofs thumping the earth like drumming.

He rides horses into town too, past the muddy Fords and Chevrolets, past the motionless men who stand like burned hemlock in front of the courthouse. At the post office boys fight to hold his horse. He gives them shiny dimes.

There are again children at the mansion, hers, two girls, dainty and clean as she was. They play croquet on the lawn or go to the lake where the father teaches them to pull the green boat with green oars over water shadowed by spruce pines. He teaches them to draw up bass from the deep, from so deep the fish are as white of belly as coal grubbers who gnaw inside the darkness of the mountain.

"She gives books to our library," Fazio, principal of the high school, says.

"There is only one Book," I say.

I study that Book at the Only Jehovah Bible College in Charleston. I ride the bus each Friday after I come out of the mountain. The city has a river which is a brown gash among smoking chemical plants, and the college is in a building which was once a tannery. It shakes with the power of our voices.

On Sunday night going home a tipsy woman sits beside me on the bus. She has bluish eyelids and a painted mouth. Her pink skirt is short, her lap smooth and satiny. In the sweeping darkness of the bus she smells of wine.

Before we reach my hollow, she laughs and touches me. With her small strong hand she does a thing. With my hand I too do a thing. When I leave the bus to step down onto the weed-lashed shoulder of the road, she sits rigid in her seat, her eyes closed, spit running from her mouth. The bus drives into blackness of the mountain, its red lights hazy through exhaust.

In blackness I go to the mountain river and strip off my clothes to wash in the healing water. I beat my flesh with stones until I bleed. I lie face up on a rock and wind flogs me. "I shall be clean," I promise the night.

Now I have children of my own, not from a wife, but from the Spirit. I feed and treat them tenderly. They lie among clean curls of wood shavings which rustle slightly. During spring and summer I harvest young rabbits hanging in my snares.

My children know me, the heat of my hand, and they raise their heads when I lower meals to them. They know my fingers when I lift them from their box. I hold them as gently as wafers.

There is a time, a day in summer. Wild flowers bloom in the fields. Scars of the rocky land are hidden by the yellow of weltering daisies. She and her daughters are picking the blooms. They come through wild grass in their colored dresses, bright like flowers themselves. I stand at the field's edge, in shadows of locust trees.

"Oh!" she says, noticing me. She is afraid. "You're Mr. . . . ?"

"Gormer," I say.

"Of course. I've head about your lay ministry at the church."

"Yes," I say.

There is a breeze off mountains that afternoon, from the south, off sunny ridges, and the breeze bends flowers and wild grass toward her, as if all those blooms are worshiping her. It is a vision I have of grass and flowers bending before her.

"Well, the church has needed a minister," she says.

Her daughters run among flowers of the field. They are hidden by blooms. Her lavender dress is blowing against her, flat against her body and curved around her legs. Along with sweetness of flowers, the breeze carries perfume off her skin to me.

"What is it?" she asks, staring at me.

Because there is a terrible bending in me too, a darkness forcing me down among flowers, my knees crushing flowers, the juice of them on my pants. Bees fly into my face. I can't lift myself but am pressed against the hot moist ground, a black hand mashing my back, my breath smothering in blooms. I raise a hand to her.

"Don't do that!" she says, stepping away, causing flowers to drag against her dress. "I'll have you arrested!"

My hand toward her, I crawl, the stalks and yellow flowers scratching my face. She gathers her running daughters from among the blooms and hurries them before her across the field. Around them bees spiral.

I lower my face to wild grass. I clutch stalks of flowers and hear bees. I weep into the yielding earth until shadows of the mountain slide over me.

"She helped with the town water," Capito says. Capito operates a Joy machine whose whirling steel teeth chew the shiny seam.

"It is not the water of life," I say.

I am an ugly man, my trunk short, my legs thick and bowed, but I've been given blessings and power. I know there will be judgment. There is always judgment.

First her husband, the army officer, goes to war. We see photographs of him in newspapers, wearing his uniform, and one picture has him on his black horse jumping a white fence, but now he lies in the darkness where no man bounds until the fiery summons of the last golden trumpet.

"He was a good fellow," Beasley, a super at the mine, says. "He talked funny, but he came to the fire company meetings."

"He would like fire," I say.

For many summers she doesn't return. She keeps Darce, the black man, up there to clean, cut hedges, and turn on the big furnace when fields grow jagged again as they shed grass and weeds. Ice scabs the mountain. Nights a light is seen—Darce and his toothless arthritic wife living in a third-floor room. The light is blackened by snow.

"She allows the children to skate on her lake," Miss Bozack, the public health nurse, says. "She sent her permission."

"She will thirst for coolness," I say.

For many summers she doesn't come until the warming afternoon when she speeds along the dusty road between the pale corn, she and her daughters, and more baggage in a second car which her secretary drives. The daughters are young ladies now, with bare arms and thin tan legs. They open windows of the mansion. That evening there are many lights.

During the summer she hires workmen and painters. She has the boathouse and bathhouse at the lake repaired, new shutters hung. Weeds are burned from the tennis court, and freshly laundered lines are nailed into clay. Squeaking sprinklers coil water over the lawn. On mown grass she has a party with music. People drive from Beckley and Bluefield to dance under oaks.

"Like old times," Puckett says, Puckett a shriveled coal grubber who, trapped in the mine, axed off his own arm to be screaming free of slate. He sits on a bottle crate and looks at colored lights among oaks on the mountain.

"You liked old times, did you?" I ask.

"They bled us," he says. "Before the union they bled us, and now the union bleeds us, but the family had style. The old man smoked dollar cigars and drove a black Packard coupe." Puckett nods. "She still has style."

"Pleasing is the face of evil," I say.

The daughters, the young ladies, do not stay long, though she invites people from cities—young men who come in toy cars. She has the stable fixed and a new float put on the lake, but it is not enough for the daughters. They want to be where there are always music, laughing, and the parading of flesh. Except for servants, she is often alone in the mansion.

"What does she do?" Ross asks. Ross owns a tin-roof store which tilts among cinders and weeds, a single peeling gas pump in front.

"She picks her flowers and sits in the shade to sew," Benita, his wife, says. Benita has helped wash windows of the mansion and with the cleaning of the heavy yellow curtains in the parlor.

"Sews?" Ross asks. "Why would she sew when she can have that and everything else done for her?"

"She likes to keep busy," Benita says. "Just like her mister would repair leather."

"Toil of Satan," I say.

I know she will come, and I wait her visit. I too am alone. My vision has set me apart. In haulways of the mine men do not set their lunch pails near me. When I walk into the cafe of the bus station, they quiet. Sundays, standing at the altar of my church, I lift my children, and the hush is so whole that I hear willow branches dragging in the stream.

I am at the church on a July morning painting eaves which rain has rotted. The air is still, though dust devils stir the corn. Crows caw over the hot land. From my ladder I look toward the mansion, dark in oak shade. I watch the blue car slide from shade.

I climb down and go inside. I know she will not be alone. Through the pointed doorway I see that Darce is driving. He is old now, white-headed, but he still struts. He wears a black tie and billed cap. The car, the blue Lincoln, stops, yet dust rolls past it and settles on grass and thistle.

I wipe sweat from my face and wait before the altar. They honk the horn as if I will leave the sanctuary at their command, as if I am a servant to run for them instead of possessing the true Word from the mouth of the Only Jehovah.

Twice more they honk, but I stand in stillness of my church, seeing dust twist in sun shafts and seeing the golden grain of oak pews I have wiped clean and laid black hymnbooks on. I see the empty oak cross.

There are footsteps and a shadow in the doorway. Darce comes. He scowls, full of pride of that family, as if he shares their blood.

"She's in the car," he says.

"She's welcome here," I say. I smile, knowing she will not come in, that holy places are forbidden her.

"She don't have to be welcome," Darce says. "She's waiting for you."

I am tempted to wrath and chastisement of this black man who swaggers in a white man's country. But I understand he too is an instrument.

She sits in the rear of her blue car, no hat on her darkly tinted hair. The window is up to keep her cool. She rolls it down, but only a little. I smell her perfume. Darce stops beside me. He is watchdog over her. She tries to be haughty like her mother.

"My grandfather set aside land for this church," she says. "He wanted it used, as do I."

"It is being used," I say.

"But not for that," she says. "They tell me—" She stops speaking. Her face creases its powder, and her bejeweled hands move on her orange lap. "I've heard—"

"What?" I ask.

"You're using the snakes," Darce says. "People talk in town."

"This church was never meant for that," she says.

She is agitated, and her hands wiggle on her lap. Her white fingers tremble. Her knees rise under her summer dress. She is afraid of me.

"In this church everything's sanctified by the Book," I say.

"Everybody knows you're using snakes," Darce says. "Somebody's going to get hurt."

"The righteous can't be hurt," I say.

"I won't have it," she says and balls her fingers. "You must stop or—"

"Or?" I ask.

"You must stop!"

I smile. She has never been inside. On Sundays she is driven more than forty miles to a heathen Bluefield church with spires, candles, and jeweled harlots. She is forbidden a truly holy place.

She rolls up her window and rolls it down again.

"I don't want to interfere," she says. "But you must stop."

"Come in and see," I say.

"She don't have to come in," Darce says.

"I hope you'll take to heart what I'm telling you," she says.

"And you better," Darce says.

I stand in dust while Darce gets in the car and drives her away. There is no breeze, and the shadows are hot. Dust palls my skin. I climb my ladder to finish painting eaves.

That night I lie awake on my cot and her perfume seeps to me. I pray, my forehead against the floor. I raise my eyes to see lightning flash among black scalloped mountains. The thunder talks to me.

Sunday I carry my sleek children to church. They have their wooden box. Cars park beneath willows and sycamores. Men stand in shade to smoke while women enter with their children to sit in the oak pews. When they see the box beside the altar, their faces tighten and gloss.

"We'll sing," I say. "We'll raise voices to the Lord."

I lead the singing. My baritone is loud and strong. Their mouths move, but they watch the box.

> Nail me to Thy cross,
> Spill Thy blood on me,
> Lower Thy thorns to cut my brow,
> Seize my soul to Thee.

After the singing, I preach. I feel myself fill with Spirit, swell with It. Heat comes into me. The people's faces are like white soil to be planted by my words.

"Believing is trusting," I say. "Believing is knowing the mighty arm of Jehovah covers and protects you."

The congregation is afraid of me and my power. Their eyes keep moving to the box. Women hold their children close.

"I want to see your belief," I tell them. "I want you to prove you have it. If you have it, all the dynamite and bombs in the world can't make a dent in you. You can feed with lions and tigers. Show God the proof by standing and coming forward to this altar!"

As I know, they do not come. They stare with glittery, unblinking eyes. I cross to the box, unlatch it, and lift a child in each hand. I hold them at the centers of their waxy beaded bodies so their tails dangle and their heads sway.

"If you have belief, you can do these things," I say and drape my white-stitched, flickering children around my neck. I hang them over my shoulders and let them slide inside my shirt. I kiss them on their coarse drifting heads.

"O ye of little faith!" I cry.

I know she will hear. Perhaps she walks through her garden to the iron gate in the stone wall and listens to my voice on the breeze. I burn the Sabbath with my words. I raise my face to her mountain.

"Those in the faith cannot be bruised!" I shout.

Monday evening when I drive to the church from the mine I find a padlock. A hasp has been screwed into the door, the screws bright in the violated wood. I see Darce's footsteps in the dust.

I drive my Ford into town, where I walk past the bus station and the closed movie theater with its boarded windows and lacy posters. I pass the barber shop, the post office, and the granite courthouse. I wait for people to speak, to take my side in righteousness, but though they know of the padlock, they will not look at me. They act as if they do not see me. She has won them.

Only Giles Hooper, the deputy, standing in brown uniform by the cannon on the courthouse lawn, speaks. His hands hang from the black cartridge belt which divides his stomach.

"Stay away from the church," he says. "Next time she'll have a warrant."

"It is my church," I say.

"You may think it's yours, but the law says the land and building still belong to the company. She's hired a preacher. You stay away."

"I am an instrument, and the Holy Spirit works through me," I say.

He would not look into my eyes.

"I do what the law makes me do," he says.

And I also do what the law makes me do, the eternal law of the Only Living God. I walk to my car. People back in shadows watch. I drive from town and among dusty corn to the stone gateposts and along the gravel which is laid white between dogwoods. I pass stone benches and red flowers growing from stone urns.

In front of the manor I stop. I walk across grass which stripes my black shoes. The guests are at the side of the house, on a flagstone terrace where a table has been set with food, bottles, silver dishes, and ice in bowls. Silver horses' heads decorate glasses stuck in yellow knitted holders.

People from cities hold glasses and talk. They pluck food from the table and spear shrimp with colored toothpicks. Their mouths are red with sauce, When they see me, they become silent.

"Mr. Gormer, leave this place," she says.

"You are damned," I tell her.

"I'll throw him out," Darce says. He wears a white jacket and carries a tray.

"Who is it?" a man asks, her man. He has graying brown hair and a brown mustache on a tanned face. He has been driving from Bluefield to play tennis and swim with her. I have seen them walking among the hemlocks.

"Mr. Gormer's leaving," she says.

"Have you ever?" a young woman, the secretary, asks. When I stare, she whitens.

"You are all damned," I say.

"I'm throwing him out," Darce says.

"I'll help," her man says.

They walk toward me, but I back across grass. Faces watch, mouths closed over words. In fright the young secretary touches her breasts.

"You are all judged and lost," I say.

Darce and her man come after me. I bump an urn. They grab me. The man's fingers are strong. I feel his strength in the ache of my arm.

"Just make him leave," she says.

There is a sound rising. Giles Hooper drives through the gateway. Lights of the police car flash red. They shove me into the cage of the rear seat where the door handles have been removed. Giles drives me into the valley, but I look back to see people on the terrace talking now, excited. With them I leave fear.

"I'll see about your car," Giles says. "You bother her again and I'll drop the jail on you."

"Do you believe you can stop the working of God's will?" I ask.

"Don't put your tongue on me," Giles says. "I'll lower the jail on you and set a rock on top."

I smile because I can call down fire to smite him, but he is not the evil. He is only her agent and is so frightened of me he twitches yellowish fingers near his bone-handled Smith and Wesson.

He takes me to my hollow and cabin where I live with my children. At night I hear them glide among clean wood shavings. I listen to them, the dry wind, and the stream, and I remember my mother keening, a sound like wind.

I do not again drive into town. I do not go to the church or the mine. I walk in the forest to collect game from my snares. I squat among ferns in damp shadows.

From shadows I see her walking with her man. She wears a red blouse which bares her arms. Her bracelets and earrings flash. She holds his hand. Under tree dusk I watch them kiss.

On a night I lie in laurel near the lake her grandfather built. His crews dynamited hemlocks and dammed a valley below the manor. He set iron deer upon planted grass. The mountain water lies still and deep.

She and her man have dined among terrace candles and stroll to the lake, she holding to his arm. There is the breeze but no ripple on the water. I watch the smoldering of fireflies and cigarettes.

She and the man switch on lights to enter the white bathhouse. They come out wearing bathing suits. Her flesh is glazed by moon. Silverish they move into dark water.

They swim. I listen to splashing and laughter. They climb the ladder onto the float where they lie under moon. I run into the forest. I run so fast I make my own wind.

I return with the box. Biting my breath, I kneel among laurel. She and her man swim in from the float. They rise from the dark water. She starts away, but he reaches after her and draws her. In moon I see him put his mouth on her. She holds to him as he unties the top of her bathing suit. He kisses her, and I whimper. Her hands are splayed over his temples. He lifts and carries her into the bathhouse. A click causes light to die.

I slip to the door and hear them inside. The black shutters are already closed. Silently I tie them with line from the boathouse. I shut off power by screwing out fuses. Kneeling on the wooden steps, I lovingly feed my children through the doorway. They flow off my palms into darkness. I pull the door closed and drop the heavy padlock into the hasp.

She and her man hear and try to switch on lights. They rattle the door. The man asks about a circuit breaker. The switch keeps clicking.

As I walk toward the forest I hear her gasp. I do not turn even at the first scream.

Sea Tides

Rufus slept late, as usual on weekends, and after waking, he lay with his hands over his eyes. He listened to gulls quarreling and the ocean smashing the sand in front of the cedar, two-story cottage, which belonged to his mother. The cottage was in the striped shade of Virginia shortleaf pines she'd insisted be left standing when the contractor—an Irishman who drank—brought his earth-moving equipment.

She'd never really trusted the contractor and had driven out from Richmond two or three times a week, in her chauffeured Chrysler, to make sure he kept to his word. She'd been unable to read blueprints, but she had bluffed the workmen into believing she could so they would do everything right.

Rufus pushed up from his bed, pulled on his bathing trunks, and went barefooted down the front steps into the living room. The idea had been for the cottage to be casual, a place to relax, but his mother had furnished it, like her Richmond home, with antiques and Persian carpets. As a result, visitors never knew which world they were in—that of the beach or the drawing room.

She still bought antiques, though the Richmond house, the beach cottage, and a garage were full of them. She loved auctions even above cards. She received a good income from Rufus's father's trust, but she usually ran through the account in ten or eleven months and had to go to Mr. Goggles at the bank for an advance on the next payment, which meant he gently invaded the corpus to make distribution.

Rufus and his sister did what they could to persuade their mother to keep down expenses, and she tried in her way, pinching at the pennies only to upset the whole delicate balance by bidding foolishly for a walnut cupboard or a spool bed. She had been married to a Southern-style Edwardian husband who believed it coarse for a woman to think about money. She had faith her men would always find funds somewhere, no matter how high the bills. Dear Mr. Goggles at the bank never failed to release her from the economic snares which annually entrapped her.

Rufus walked through French doors onto a flagstone terrace, where his mother sat in the shade of a yellow-and-white beach umbrella. She wore blue silk coolie clothes and a coolie hat as wide as her shoulders. She was sorting shells, which clinked against the metal table. She would display her best specimens on dark folded paper in the den. She took her collection seriously and was often solemn over it. "Watch out for bluebottles," she said to Rufus as he kissed her cheek. She did not look up from a sand dollar she was examining. By bluebottles she meant Portuguese men-of-war. "Mr. Boatwright saw one this morning in front of the hotel."

Mr. Boatwright owned the hotel, the only one on a three-mile stretch of coast, a large, white frame building that had been constructed before Richmond people came to put up their cottages and was nearly always empty. The summer residents went there for square dancing and country-style meals, at which everybody dressed, but not too much, eating with a spirit of camaraderie. Mr. Boatwright also delivered the morning paper to green tubular boxes along the road.

"Offshore wind," Rufus said. He was in his middle thirties, though he appeared older. Lean, his black hair turning gray, he was still muscled from his swimming and racing days, but those muscles were softening. Except for his weekends here, he got little exercise. Moreover, now that he lived alone, he wasn't eating properly. "They set their sails."

"Nasty things," his mother said, wrinkling her nose and picking up a bit of lace coral. She had been a very striking woman once, having glossy black hair and skin absolutely fair, like the cleanest sand. She was still tall, even regal when she wished to be, and often in certain lights Rufus saw the ghost of lost beauty haunting her in spite of her white hair and corroding lines.

He had driven from Richmond the night before, Friday, and meant to let himself in without waking her. She, however, had been out. He had waited, drinking a Scotch and sitting on the screened porch, which faced the ocean. He'd been tired after a particularly bad week of work, on top of carrying the weight of his loneliness. When his mother finally came, she arrived in a yellow Dodge driven by a Mr. Dementi, who was wearing evening clothes. They'd been to a yacht-club dance.

Rufus had shaken hands with Mr. Dementi, a short, ruddy man with a bald head and a white mustache. Later Rufus and his mother had fixed a drink in the kitchen. She had explained Mr. Dementi was staying up the beach.

Now she frowned as she exchanged the coral for a squilla claw. Her manner was imperial. Occasionally, however, she became quite sentimental, weeping in a ladylike fashion over some faint, lost anniversary. Then, of course, she was thinking of her dead husband, Rufus's father.

"Sis coming?" Rufus asked as he stepped down from the terrace to the hot beach sand.

"This afternoon. And Mr. Dementi's having lunch with us."

Rufus stopped to look at her. She glanced at him, but her face was shaded by the coolie hat. Rufus's impression of Mr. Dementi was not favorable. Dementi's hand had felt wetly pudgy, and he had been quick to laugh in what seemed almost servile fashion.

"What's going on behind my back?" Rufus asked, teasing.

"You're not my keeper," his mother answered, her small, bowed lips forming a pout. It was a reaction Rufus hadn't expected.

"I'm going swimming," he said, and walked down the beach toward the ocean, which under the fierce sun was like molten silver. He dropped his towel, ran into the water, and dived when it reached his knees.

Swimming, he thought about his mother. She was fifty-six, and going out with men, especially during the summer when old beaux came from Richmond, wasn't unusual for her. They called her to play bridge, have dinner, go dancing, but they were connected with families who had been at the beach for years, and in most cases they had been friends of Rufus's father. Rufus had never heard of Dementi. Still, the man must be all right to be staying at one of the cottages. There were certain unwritten rules about guests along the three-mile stretch.

Rufus swam harder. At Washington & Lee he had been on the swimming team, and he was vain about his style of moving through the rough, foaming ocean, timing his strokes so that his body turned slightly and his mouth rose from the water on the crest of waves. He swam against the pull of the tide to have more of a challenge, to prove he hadn't gone entirely flabby from a suffocating office life, sure that people under colored umbrellas along the beach were watching and remarking what a good swimmer he was.

A flicker of unnatural light stopped him. He lifted his head, felt a surge of fear, and backwatered frantically. In front of him, bobbing on the waves, was an evil beauty, a bluebottle, its transparent bladder fat, its great, thick blue streamers coiling in the current like a woman's hair—delicate, languid tentacles floating out to kill and digest. Rufus thrashed away, no longer thinking of form but only survival and escape. He ran from the water to the beach, where he sat and leaned his head between his knees to catch his breath.

The sun dried him, and he thought how the bluebottle's streamers had reminded him of a woman's hair, of Lois's on a pillow, though hers was light brown, and he remembered the weekends they had spent at this beach. He remembered her in their house too, but here in the golden sun the memories were mostly good because they'd never fought at the beach. She was now in Florida with their four-year-old son, and she was about to remarry—a real estate salesman who held a record for catching a tarpon on a fly rod.

Just before she and Rufus had called it quits, they had been able to think only of getting away. They had hurt each other automatically, by reflex, as if words were knives driven into the body to destroy. They had gone through a six-week session with a marriage counselor, who had called them immature and headstrong. They'd meekly agreed, but the marriage had continued to fall apart—like a plane losing pieces of itself, wings, wheels, engines, before crashing.

After she was finally gone, after the great numbness and weariness lifted, loneliness had settled onto him, adding another burden to his struggles to keep the coffee business alive. Often he lay on the bed in his apartment, dusty in spite of maid service, among furniture from a house now sold, feeling aged and over the hill. He called it pulling out the barbs, and he wondered whether the pain would ever end. He worried that he might be stricken in some manner and not found for days, not even missed. He imagined himself lying dead and his body gathering dust . . .

He stood and headed back to his mother's cottage. Because of sand sticking to him, he showered outside before going upstairs, where he changed into a white sport shirt, tan slacks, and leather sandals. He had breakfast in the kitchen with Mattie, the colored cook his mother always brought from Richmond.

"Who's Mr. Dementi?" Rufus asked.

"He's staying at the hotel," Mattie answered. She scrubbed an iron skillet with a dab of steel wool.

Rufus put down his cup. While the beach people ate and danced at the hotel, none of them or their friends stayed there. The rooms were tiny, primitive, with poor ventilation. Mr. Dementi could be anybody at all.

"Does he come here to the cottage often?" Rufus asked.

"Not more than every day," Mattie answered and laughed. She had her own men, who drove by for her at dark and waited under the pines, never blowing their horns or even coming to the door. She was in her forties, a wiry black woman not at all pretty, but the men liked her for her good humor. She glanced at Rufus slyly, causing him to think she and his mother were in conspiracy.

He carried the morning newspaper to the terrace. His mother was still working with her shells. She was intent, sitting forward on the cushioned wrought-iron chair and whispering to herself. He pretended to read but studied her around the edge of the newspaper. He saw that she had been primping. Her nails were painted, she'd recently had her hair done, and she was using a trace of blue eye-shadow, which she sometimes did in Richmond but never at the beach.

She looked at a silver watch she wore on a silver chain around her neck and stood to scrape shells into cardboard boxes labeled with her fine handwriting.

"Leaving me?" he asked.

"I want to freshen up," she said.

When she reappeared thirty minutes later, she had on a pink dress trimmed with white around the collar, and high-heeled white shoes. She wore a string of pearls. She was perfumed and powdered. She carried a silver vase with a rose in it, which she placed on the table. All the seriousness of the shell collecting was gone, and she hummed to herself.

"If that's freshening up, I'd hate to see you put on the dog," Rufus said.

"Mr. Dementi's used to dressing," she said. She arranged chairs and sat on the glider. She smoothed her fluted skirt. "In fact, he's old fashioned."

"What's he do?"

"Something in tobacco," she said and laughed. "You know you're acting a little like a nervous parent."

She walked to the kitchen to talk to Mattie about lunch. Rufus watched the gulls sail and stall against the breeze. Their cries were like rusty gates squeaking. In spite of his long sleep, he was still tired. There was a good chance the family coffee business would fail, a development which not only would create a mess in itself but also would mean that he would have to start over. At his age he could hardly be expected to look forward to that.

Mr. Dementi arrived at exactly one o'clock. He was driving the yellow Dodge. He had on white flannel trousers, a red-and-white striped blazer, and a Panama hat. His ruddy skin jarred with his white mustache. He was at least sixty. Holding his Panama hat under his arm, he came up the terrace steps like a person familiar with the way.

"Hello there again!" he called and smiled, showing teeth too perfect to be anything except false. Rufus shook his hand. Dementi was short, yet held himself erectly. He had a habit of touching his mustache, as if he were about to twirl the points in the manner of a hussar.

Rufus used the few minutes he had before his mother came out. He and Dementi sat on the flowered glider, which faced the ocean. Dementi held his Panama hat squarely on his lap.

"How'd you happen to discover the hotel?" Rufus asked, hoping the question didn't sound like an interrogation.

"I do things like this quite often," Dementi explained. "I spread out a map and study it until I find an interesting-looking spot—you know, with more than ordinary land conformation—restricting myself, of course, to the coast, because I love the sea. I noticed this stretch because if you hold your map just right, the point of land north of here resembles a dragon's head."

Rufus had never looked at the map in that way, though he did later, and Dementi was right about the dragon's head.

Dementi said he'd driven along the coast, staying as near the ocean as possible, and just chanced on the hotel.

"It's a period piece," he said enthusiastically. "Some of the rooms have porcelain water pitchers and washbowls. It's like going back to a time when the ladies carried parasols and the men wore swimming suits like longjohns and did the breast stroke so they wouldn't wet their mustaches."

"I understand you're in tobacco," Rufus just had time to say. He heard his mother coming through the cottage.

"I was president of a small company in Winston-Salem," Dementi answered. "We did a leaf-export-type business but couldn't stand against the giants. Now I'm more or less retired, though I do have investment interests."

Rufus's mother walked out, her steps quick and hard on the flagstones, her jeweled hand extended to Dementi. He stood so quickly Rufus half expected him to click his heels.

Rufus thought how pretty his mother was when she was animated and how men Dementi's age would consider her quite a dish. Rufus noticed Dementi held her hand in both of his.

"I have gimlets," his mother said. "Mattie's bringing them out."

Rufus was fascinated by his mother, who acted girlish and kept standing during lunch to wait on Dementi, urging on him shrimp, cheese, and more gray trout. Each time she stood, Dementi did also, so they were popping up and down like comic opera. Their conversation had a breathless quality, as if one of them were about to board a plane.

After lunch Rufus excused himself to go to his room. For a while he read a paperback novel, one from his mother's pile. Out on the terrace he heard bursts of laughter. He walked to a window in the hall, stood back from the gauzy white curtain, and watched.

His mother and Dementi were sitting on the glider. Dementi reached over and placed a hand on her crossed knee. As Rufus sucked in his breath, she lowered her hands on top of Dementi's and pressed his there.

Rufus's sister came after Dementi left, in her large station wagon loaded with golden-haired children, who were brown from daily swims at the country club. They wanted to go into the water immediately. Rufus walked them to the ocean and let them play in the surf. He was on guard against bluebottles.

After a while his sister joined him. She was an athletic-looking blonde and wore a flaming pink two-piece bathing suit. She settled on one of the colored beach towels they called Joseph's coats.

"Mother has a beau," Rufus said.

"Really?" his sister asked, not disturbed. She rubbed oil on herself. Her pretty brown legs were crossed yoga fashion. She was married to a broker, and in the pursuit of society, they lived beyond their means. Alf, her husband, had notes at several banks.

"She was playing coy and holding hands," Rufus went on.

"Mother?" his sister said, squinting into the sunlight and twisting the cap back on the plastic tube of oil.

"I'll see what I can find out," Rufus told her.

After dinner that evening, he pretended he was going for a stroll, but walked the sandy road to the hotel. With just a few alterations, the white frame building could have been changed into a Western saloon. In the lobby were fanbacked wicker chairs and dried-out fish, mounted by Mr. Boatwright. The lobby was empty, though some of the cottagers were in the dining room.

Rufus found Mr. Boatwright on the front porch, where he sat with a foot cocked on the salt-rusted iron railing.

Mr. Boatwright had once been a commercial fisherman, and he could listen to the gull cries and tell when the blues were running. He was near eighty, but still lean and weathered. He had his own teeth, yellowed by tobacco.

"He keeps to himself and don't do much talking," Mr. Boatwright said when, later, Rufus steered the conversation to Dementi.

"That so?" Rufus asked, thinking it certainly was not the way Dementi acted at the cottage.

"He blew a fuse pressing his pants. I had to tell him he couldn't use an iron up there."

Rufus wondered about a man with investment interests also carrying his own iron.

"He nips," Mr. Boatwright, who was a Baptist, went on. "He sits up there alone in his room and nips out of a bottle."

Rufus frowned. He pictured the little man sitting in shorts and undershirt on the edge of a narrow bed, sweating and lifting the bottle.

"Anyway he's leaving tomorrow," Mr. Boatwright said.

"Are you sure?" Rufus asked, shifting in his chair.

"He told me to have his bill ready," Mr. Boatwright said.

Dementi came to the cottage the next morning, but his visit turned out to be a farewell. Relieved that this was the end of it, Rufus tried to be cordial, as did his sister, whom Rufus had talked to after returning from the hotel.

Their mother had breakfast served on the terrace, a merry affair with wine and laughter as Dementi told a long story about how he'd gone big-game hunting in Africa and been chased up a baobab tree by a grunting warthog. He handled the story well, and their mother put her hand to her throat and became wet eyed as she laughed. Rufus thought again of Dementi's drinking alone in the hot monkish room of the hotel.

While Rufus and his sister stayed on the terrace, their mother and Dementi spoke their private good-by under the shadows of the pines. Rufus did not spy on them, though it was thirty minutes before the yellow Dodge drove off and his mother came back. Smiling, she touched her hair. She insisted they have another glass of wine.

She didn't tell Rufus and his sister until late afternoon. She sat them in the antique-filled living room and paced in front of the fireplace, which had driftwood stacked in it. She kept clasping and unclasping her hands. Her jewelry rattled. "I've something to discuss," she said, and she frowned. Rufus and his sister stared at her. She cleared her throat. "I've been lonely since your father died. I've tried not to worry you, but at times I've been depressed."

She paced in front of them, becoming increasingly nervous and unsure, while Rufus and his sister sat motionless on the Queen Anne sofa, knowing what was next, yet refusing to help. Their mother wouldn't look them in the eye.

"I loved your father dearly, and always will, but this has nothing to do with him. I'm thinking of marrying Leonard Dementi."

Before Rufus or his sister could speak, their mother hurried on. Apparently she had thought out what she wanted to say.

"Now don't protest," she told them, holding up a hand as if to ward them off. "I haven't definitely made up my mind. Leonard and I agreed we've known each other only a short time and should do nothing impetuous. That's his wish as well as mine. We've decided to spend a month away from each other. Then he'll come back, and we'll make a decision."

She was so nervous she trembled and repeatedly pushed at her hair. She looked at Rufus and his sister obliquely.

"I feel I've been hit on the head with a brick," the sister said, more to herself than to them, and reached for a cigarette. The cigarettes were in a silver dish on the parqueted coffee table.

"I don't have so many years left," their mother said. "I'd like a little more happiness."

They talked about it off and on through the rest of the afternoon and evening. At times they argued, and there were attempts at reason. Once Rufus and his sister whispered in the darkness of the

back stairs. They were concerned about their mother and certainly desired her happiness. They agreed, however: they were afraid of Dementi.

Moreover, though neither Rufus nor his sister ever talked of their mother's money eventually passing to them, they were thinking about it. They hoped she would live to be a hundred, but when she did die, they wanted what was theirs. They sensed they would need it.

Their mother wouldn't listen to them. They saw she had made up her mind. The month's cooling-off period meant nothing. When Rufus went to bed late that night, his mother and sister were still at it.

"You don't know anything about him!" the sister said for what must have been the thousandth time.

"I know he's gentle. I've come to value that above most things."

"But you can't be sure."

"I have you and Rufus so little. You ought to understand I need someone."

Rufus believed he had to protect his mother, yet he wasn't certain how to go about it. Then, driving back to Richmond early Monday morning, he thought of using a private detective. He looked up agencies in the yellow pages, chose the first in a list of five, and talked with a Mr. Kermit Lilly over the telephone. That afternoon at three, Rufus left his warehouse office to drive uptown to see Mr. Lilly.

Lilly was a large, freckled man who spoke as if thinking over each word before allowing it to leave his mouth. He wore a dark undertaker's suit and spoke barely above a whisper. Rufus had the impression Lilly was from the backcountry but had doggedly slicked over himself a veneer of civilization. On the brown wall behind him was a color photograph of J. Edgar Hoover.

When Lilly finished taking down the few details Rufus knew about Dementi, he leaned back in an executive pose and spoke in funereal tones.

"Just how thorough an investigation do you want?"

"It's important to my family you find out all you can about him,"

Rufus said.

"We'll find out all there is," Lilly said.

After leaving the agency, Rufus went by the bank to talk to Mr. Goggles, the officer who handled his mother's business affairs. Rufus's father had set up a trust under a will, directing that she have the use and benefit of the estate during her life and that at her death the residue be divided between Rufus and his sister. If their mother married Dementi, he might use her to milk the principal.

"Your father expressly stated she be allowed to invade the corpus," Mr. Goggles, a grave, deliberate man who acted like a member of the family, said, telling Rufus what he already knew. "I can advise her, of course, but she has a right to the money if she insists."

On each of the next two Fridays, Rufus went to the beach to attempt to persuade his mother to change her mind. He had convinced himself and his sister that Dementi was an adventurer. Rufus tried not to think that he wanted Dementi to be so.

Rufus's mother smiled and patted his hand, but she would not listen. She was living within herself. She had put away her shells, stacking the boxes in a downstairs closet. She was happily buying a wardrobe—dresses and gowns, which lay across her tester bed and brought slashes of color to her shaded room. Sitting before a mirror, she tried on hats and made faces at herself.

During the third week, Rufus received a report from Lilly at the detective agency. The report was in a brown folder and neatly typed. Most of the information was routine—date of birth, parents, schools, and college—but a few items were disturbing.

For example, Dementi had been married twice, the second time to a woman much younger than he, a nightclub dancer, who was still collecting alimony. Moreover, his tobacco business had not simply folded but had been declared bankrupt. Creditors had not received ten cents on the dollar, and a good bit of ill feeling still existed among them. Lastly, Dementi was living off capital, selling parcels of real estate left him by his father, which, as far as Lilly could determine, were the only assets he owned other than a small checking account in a Winston-Salem bank and the yellow Dodge.

Rufus and his sister agreed he should go see Dementi, and on Thursday Rufus flew from Richmond to Winston-Salem. He took a taxi to the address listed in the detective report, an apartment built in the Spanish style of the 'twenties, fashionable once, but now run down, decaying, with cracks in the enormous stone flowerpots flanking the doorway and rust on the grillework. The elevator was out of order.

Dementi lived on the fourth floor. Rufus knocked, and while he waited looked down the mustard-colored corridor, where children had scribbled their names on the walls. When the door opened, Dementi was bewildered. He then recovered and held out his hand. From inside the apartment came the smell of frying fish.

Dementi had on an unpressed red sportshirt, gray slacks, and an apron. "You've caught me," he said, stepping back to allow Rufus to enter. "I'm cooking. It's one of the things I do. I've always wanted to be a chef."

He was embarrassed about Rufus seeing the apartment, which was merely a living room, a small bedroom, and a kitchen too tiny to hold even a table. The furniture was incipiently shabby, as if nothing new had been purchased for years. The living room was crowded with ragtag memories of other times—tennis rackets and sabers in a corner, photographs of college days, a rowing oar, a snapshot of Dementi on a glistening black horse, receiving a silver trophy from a judge. The trophy was there too, though it needed shining, and tarnish obscured the engraving.

"Please sit down," Dementi said, hurrying to the kitchen. He turned off the stove, untied his apron, and came back, pushing a hand over his ruddy scalp. The apartment was hot, and he was sweating.

"I don't think you'll want me to sit," Rufus said. He handed Dementi a copy of Lilly's report. The original was in a safe-deposit box of the Richmond bank.

Dementi, puzzled, reached for his glasses and leafed rapidly through the pages until he understood. He lowered himself slowly to a splitting leather chair and read while Rufus stood by a dusty window and looked toward a distant television tower. The tower had a red light on it. Pigeons sailed around the steel ribs, their wings catching the sun as they banked to land.

"All right," Dementi said when he finished reading. Tossing the report to a sofa, he stood. His face was redder than ever. His cheeks puffed and his white mustache trembled. "What do you want from me?"

"Nothing," Rufus answered. "Nothing at all."

"Why should I listen to you?" Dementi asked. He walked around the leather chair, a furious small man whose voice quivered. "It's between your mother and me."

"I'll show her the report. She has a different idea of you. She thinks you're practically nobility."

Dementi sank to the worn, old-fashioned sofa, which under his weight weakly spiraled dust into the hot light. Leaning back, he closed his eyes. He looked feeble and tired. Rufus felt sorry for him. We both live alone, he thought. We have that in common. Dementi ran a shaky, veined hand over his sweating face. He spoke without opening his eyes.

"Have you ever considered the fact I might honestly love your mother?"

"Maybe, but you're too risky."

"She'll marry me anyway," he said. He opened his eyes and pushed himself up, rocking slightly on his feet.

"She may, but it won't be the same after this report."

Dementi's mouth turned down, and again he puffed his shiny, rosy cheeks. Straightening his shoulders, he walked to the door, which he opened.

"Get out," he said. "Just get the hell out."

Rufus drove to the beach at the end of the month, a hot Saturday afternoon when traffic was a sluggish snake coiling upon itself. He was drained from another week's struggle at the coffee company. A final decision had to be made soon. The board of directors expected a recommendation from him, and that recommendation would inevitably be a signpost pointing to his own failure to revive the business.

His best hope was to be allowed to resign without a family row and bitterness. More than those even, he dreaded the effort which would be required of him to establish a new life. He was no longer sure he had the guts to start over.

On the drive to the cottage, he switched his thinking from one set of worries to another. Neither he nor his sister was certain what Dementi had done or would do as a result of the report. Possibly he had already seen their mother and alibied himself, though Rufus doubted that. There would have been some reaction from the mother, who had not written or called.

The cottage was full of flowers his mother had cut in her garden, every vase and bowl sweet and colorful. Rufus kissed her. She wore a lavender dress and moved about humming. The more he watched her, the more certain he was she knew nothing of the report. She hurried about the cottage, punching pillows and arranging more flowers, as fluttery as a young girl before her first cotillion.

Rufus's sister had arrived earlier. When their mother's back was turned, he looked at his sister questioningly. She raised her hands palms upward and pointed to the dining room table, which had been set for four.

"He must be coming," she whispered as soon as their mother was beyond earshot. "At least she assumes it."

Rufus had a swim and a shower before dressing and joining his mother and sister on the terrace. Mattie, in a white uniform, served drinks from a silver tray.

The mother chatted about the high water they'd had during the week, the result of a northeaster that had washed away part of her beach. Each time a car came along the road, she turned her head expectantly. She told them that, at the height of the storm, a young dolphin had washed up on the sand. She and the other cottagers had pushed it back into the ocean.

After the second drink, the brass ship's clock on the den wall struck seven, and Mattie came from the kitchen to ask about dinner.

"We'll wait a while longer," the mother said. "He's been delayed."

They waited another forty-five minutes. By then their mother had begun to play nervously with her pearls, twisting her fingers in the strands. There were lapses in the conversation during which the ocean seemed to break with unusual force, shaking the ground. The ebbing light of the sun made a golden web in the sky.

At last their mother stood. "We may as well eat," she said. "He's been detained."

At dinner she acted the part of a hostess, not looking at the empty chair and talking rapidly to cover her alarm. When the telephone rang, she hurried to answer it, reaching the walnut stand in the hall before Mattie could walk from the kitchen.

"This will be Leonard," their mother called back to the dining room.

Rufus and his sister sat with their hands in their laps, eying each other while their mother talked. It wasn't Dementi on the telephone, but another widow, an arthritic old dowager who was also a shell collector. She was having a tea Tuesday afternoon at four. Rufus's mother said she wasn't going to be here Tuesday.

She returned to the dining room. For a moment she stood quietly, her jeweled white hands on top of her chair. Then she laughed.

"Do you suppose I've been jilted?" she asked.

"Have you heard from him?" Rufus asked.

"I didn't think I had to hear from him." She sat. She was brave. She held up her head and talked about people at the beach. After dinner they followed her to the screened-in porch. They had coffee and looked at the ghostly phosphorescence of the ocean. Their mother said she was thinking of having a seawall built. She was corresponding with several contractors, asking them to bid on the work.

In the middle of a sentence, she stood, said good night, and left the porch. Her bed was on the first floor, in a large room that had been prepared for the father when he had his first angina attack. Lights from the window shone on crape myrtle and on sea oats in front of the cottage.

"I'm going to tell her," the sister said, crying silently.

Rufus refused to let her go. He argued that a little pain now would save a great deal more later—pain for all of them. In whispers they talked about it. Finally the sister stopped crying, wiped at her eyes, and walked listlessly upstairs to bed.

Rufus had a drink before going to his room, which was over his mother's. When he switched off his bedside lamp, he saw her lights were still on. They caused shadows among the sea oats, waving bars of darkness against the sand.

He couldn't sleep. He worried about his mother, telling himself he had done the right thing, yet unable to kill doubt. He worried as well about Dementi, who was not greatly different from himself. He tossed on the bed, reached for a cigarette, and walked to the window. The ocean was dark except for a shaft of gold laid on the water by the moon.

His mother's light was still burning. In a lull of waves he heard the rustling of tissue paper and the sound of drawers being shut. He stood looking at the ocean and weakening, thinking his sister had been right about telling their mother. He could at least comfort her. He drew on his bathrobe, but as he was fastening the belt, his mother's shadow swept across the yellow patch of sand and sea oats, and her light went out.

In the morning when he woke, he heard clinking. He hurried along the hall. His sister, clutching at her white robe, was already at the window. Their mother sat at the table on the terrace. She had on her coolie clothes. From small boxes she was taking shells, squilla claws, and sand dollars, which she arranged before her.

As Rufus and his sister watched, their mother stopped and was still a moment, squinting toward the sea as if she'd heard a call. Then, like a person suffering an inner rebuke, she quickly returned to sorting her shells.

The Darkened Room

In the late winter light Richard lay slanted on the hard cold slope and watched the house. Scrub oaks around him were nearly stripped, but a few straggling leaves spun on the wind and dryly tapped the frozen ground.

The yellow house was new, two stories with a bronze television antenna whose glinting spikes and grids spanned most of the white shingle roof. At the rear was a swimming pool, covered now by a green plastic sheet which had trapped rain and leaves in its sagging center.

During the late summer he'd walked through gray gritty air of the industrial West Virginia valley and crossed the black iron bridge over the slate Kanawha River. He climbed from haze to sunlight. He carried a sickle while he eyed the houses beyond shaped hedges and rustic stone walls splotched with pale lichen.

There were certain conditions. The house must show money and could have no children or dogs. The people had to go out often. And he required a place he'd be able to approach from the rear by hiking through a rocky hollow too sheer for dwellings.

He'd climbed among scrub oaks of the hollow before leaves fell. The last locusts broke off their feeble chirring. From the ridge he studied the neighborhood. The yellow house was without a swing set or bicycle. No children jumped into the glossy pool. A thin blonde wearing a pink halter and shorts walked barefooted across new grass. She smoked and read a magazine in the sunshine beside the pool, but she never went into the water.

The chunky balding man came home late when the evenings were too cool to swim. He put on faded denims and a checked wool shirt. Holding a drink, he paced around the spotlighted concrete apron, arranged the colored deck chairs, and vacuumed the bottom of the pool. He poured chemicals into the water. Finally he covered the pool with the green plastic sheet.

Richard sneaked away from high school to watch at different hours. Except weekends, the man left for work after fixing his own breakfast. He drove a red Cadillac he kept in a garage that had electric doors. When he went down the hill, the fat tires slicked against the damp asphalt. Later the woman wearing a rose housecoat sat in the kitchen to drink coffee, smoke, and watch television.

She had her own car, a blue Chevy with a white vinyl top. A cigarette in her mouth, she'd hose off the car and leave it dripping in the sunshine. Sometimes she pulled weeds around shrubs or poked at flowers. She carried her cigarettes and lighter but stayed at the job only a few minutes. She didn't really care about the flowers.

They had parties. People drank and danced on flagstones or beside the pool. Music played from a phonograph set on a white metal table. At a party a couple hiked up the slope through darkness to the scrub oaks and lay close to Richard. The woman raised her hips so the man could lift her swishing, ghostly dress and settle the skirt across her throat. Down at the pool another woman called for her husband amid laughter.

The couple who owned the yellow house went out every Saturday they didn't give a party themselves. Once they hadn't come in on Sunday morning. The milk and newspaper arrived before they did. Wearing a tuxedo, the man staggered from his Caddy and hit golf balls from the rear lawn up the slope. He lurched, cut sod, and sliced a ball which thunked against an oak.

Richard was tensed to stand and run, but the man never came after the balls. He fell, and his wife in a silver gown tried to help him. She also was drunk. They both fell. Crawling to the house, they tracked the dew.

"Got to get some practice for the tournament," the man said.

When Richard left the apartment to cross the bridge and climb the hill to the yellow house, he lied to his mother. He told her he was going to the gym to shoot baskets. She was a nurse. She rubbed her feet, stared out of the garage-apartment window toward the river, and accused Richard's father who'd abandoned them. In more than seven years she'd heard from him only once, a card postmarked Tombstone. On the front was a picture of a giant green cactus. There was no message or signature, and the penciled address had smeared, but she was certain the father had sent it.

"He carried off everything except the bills," she said. "He didn't leave me change to ride the bus to the hospital. He took my keys and cigarettes. He took the opal ring my own mother willed me."

"You were always at him," Richard said. He remembered the hateful voices in the night.

"I was at him?" she asked, raising her arms. "He cheated me out of my life. He lied, robbed, and gave me a filthy disease from his whoring, and you tell me I was at him? I wish I'd killed him. I wish I could put a knife in him right now. And you're like him!"

On summer nights the rounded hills blocked any breeze, and the valley was thick and fiery. Richard and his mother had to sit on the small porch to breathe. He'd unroll his mattress over the dry grass beside the garage and lie looking up through haze to flickering lights on the hills which were like great combers about to crash on him from a dark sea. He wanted them to wash him out of the valley.

Even when he pretended to sleep, his mother's accusing voice swathed him. She said he had his father in him and that she expected him to betray her. He was sick to puking of what older people had done to his world. He wanted away, and away to him was California and the cold cleansing Pacific surf to which he transformed the hills in the hot choking cocoon of his mother's voice.

On a Saturday during October, the night of the year's first killing frost, he waited until the couple left, slipped from the scrub oaks, and walked crouched down the slope to the darkened end of the yellow house. He touched the painted siding as if meaning would come through it to him. He backed over flagstones, climbed the slope, and let his breathing quiet before hiking down along the black hollow where leaves crackled.

Another night he carried some of his father's old tools from the garage apartment to the slope—a hammer, a screwdriver, a crowbar, and a hacksaw. He wrapped polyethylene around the tools and buried them under the fringe of a laurel bush. The top of the ground was so frozen he chipped at it with the screwdriver until he reached soil soft enough to claw out.

By December he was ready. He'd been on the cold slope since late afternoon. Strung around his neck by the laces were his basketball shoes. The purplish winter light deepened to darkness. Wind gusted from the valley, and he smelled factory smoke and river mud. He heard the whistle of a diesel tug pushing coal barges. He dug up the tools.

The couple were dressing and passed bright windows of their bedroom. The woman in a red gown which bared her arms and back turned before a mirror. The man went downstairs for another drink. He wore his tuxedo and put on a white scarf and black overcoat.

He walked through the kitchen to the garage. He switched on a spotlight over the entrance, and the bulb steamed in the cold. The white door whirred up. As he started the Caddy's engine, he honked. The woman hurried down the steps and through the house to the garage. She wore red slippers, a fur, and a golden kerchief over her blonde hair. When the Caddy was out, the garage door slid closed.

Richard watched the red taillights dip behind the wall. He waited. The woman might have forgotten a purse or gloves and make the man return. Most of the downstairs windows were lighted, as was the bedroom end of the upstairs. He listened to traffic on the hill road. The moon laid a pale sheen on the house and grass. Still he waited. He ran in place to keep warm.

Finally he changed from his brogans to his basketball shoes. He tied double knots. He passed his belt through the loop of the hacksaw blade. The rest of the tools he stuck under his belt. He set his brogans beside the laurel bush. The flashlight he held in his left hand. When he moved down the slope, his feet crunched frozen grass.

He approached the house from the darkest side. He walked among stirring shrubs and past the snapping plastic cover over the pool. On flagstones his basketball shoes made a sticky noise like adhesive tape being removed.

He stared through a storm window that had ice crystals around the glass's edge. The living room furniture was modern and shiny. An outsized yellow sofa was marked with tiger stripes. Brass platters hung on walls. The white Formica bar had a brass rail and chrome stools.

He skirted the spotlight. He could have broken any window, but it was easier to go through the garage because that window had no storm sash. He pulled at the cuffs of the brown cotton gloves he'd bought from Woolworth's, tested the small window by pushing up against it, and drew his hammer from his belt. With a single slight tap he smashed the pane under the latch.

The sound of the glass was like wind chimes. He stuck the hammer into his belt, reached through the broken pane, and unfastened the latch. He waited while a car passed on the road. Slowly he raised the window.

The new wood was tight and squeaky. He brushed chips of glass into a pile at the side of the sill. He gripped the sill, jumped to it, and dropped into the lighted garage. He started away but went back to close the window.

He walked around the rear of the glittering blue Chevy. He hoped the woman had been so hurried she hadn't locked the door into the house. He turned the knob, and the door opened onto a shadowy utility room which smelled of wetness and soap. Beyond were stainless steel and avocado fixtures of the kitchen.

The kitchen and other rooms had red, yellow, and orange wall-to-wall carpets which were springy under his feet. He hurried through the first floor. He would take no silver, furs, or television sets. Whatever he stole must be easily carried not only down to the valley and the bus station, but also to California, where he could safely sell or hock it.

He ran up the carpeted steps to the couple's blue bedroom. The ceiling light was still switched on, as were lamps with white metal shades shaped like cones above the mirrored dressing table. The bed was circular and had a yellow coverlet.

At the foot was a color television on a golden tubular stand. Across a blue chaise longue the woman had thrown a bra and a crumpled pair of panty hose. An ashtray on the blond chest of drawers was heaped and still smoldering.

He went first to the dressing table. He fingered clinking bottles. He pushed aside powder, perfume, and eyelash curlers. He felt into grainy rears of drawers. He found a ruby bow of costume jewelry.

He stepped over the man's soiled underwear to the blond chest. He pulled out drawers and shuffled shirts, blouses, and sacheted lingerie. He discovered pocketbooks, but each was empty. In the bottom drawer was a lacy white nightgown. Under it lay a black automatic pistol. He searched around, yet didn't touch it.

He went to the closets. He patted dresses and the man's suits and jackets. He felt into shoes. He rubbed his gloved palms across the floor and pushed fingers into dusty corners. He stood on a slick red ottoman and lifted hats and boxes from a shelf.

He patted the bed and worked a hand beneath pillows and mattress. On his back he kicked himself under the bed. Lint fell on his face, and he sneezed. He ran his fingers along slats.

He jerked prints of exotic flowers from the walls in hope of finding a safe. He went to the flamingo bathroom and raised bottles from the medicine cabinet. He ruffled towels in the linen closet. A wad of woman's blonde hair lay curled around the drain of the flamingo tub.

He walked quickly along the hall and shined his flashlight into the next room. His fingers curved over the lens divided the beam into strips. It was a guest room. Except for blankets, sheets, and empty picture frames, the drawers held nothing. Summer clothes hung in the closet.

He went to the last room, the one at the dark end of the house. As he closed his hand on the knob, he heard honking and turned. No car drove up the drive. He opened the door and held the flashlight ahead of him.

For an instant he believed he'd come to judgment. On a throne at the center of the room was massed a dark figure with phosphorescent eyes. Richard tasted vomit and almost fouled himself.

Like an explosion, light erupted. He covered his face and whimpered. He waited to be struck dead. Slowly he lowered his arms and stared at the figure—a fat old woman who sat in a high-backed cane wheelchair.

She bulged through the chair, and it dented her flesh. She wore a black, powder-dusted dress which had buttons missing, cotton stockings, and flowered bedroom slippers that were split along the seams. Her legs were as thick at the ankles as at the knees. Creases of her face were so deep they held shadows. On her neck was a growth which lapped over her white collar to her shoulder. Kinks of white hair grew from a flaking pinkish scalp. Her green eyes had chips of darkness in them. Her lashes and brows were gone.

"For a thief you hardly got fuzz on you," she said.

A fat hand was still raised to the waxy shade of a floor lamp. The hand bumped the shade. Her head was palsied. A fleck of spit glistened on her square outthrust chin. The spit was brown. She tightened her bottom lip over a lump he guessed was snuff.

"How'd you get here?" he asked. He was weak and greasy with sweat.

"Why I been here," she said. "Men carried me up the stairs, and here I been."

Her talk was hillbilly. He'd heard enough of it at school, the reluctant words of the quiet sullen children who came on muddy yellow busses from the dismal hollows. The shy girls moved in clumps. The boys carried bone-handled knives, and a towhead had attacked an English teacher who tried to discipline him for tearing pages out of a literature book. The teacher, a middle-aged man, had fled the classroom.

"I'd have seen you," Richard said.

"How would you seen me?" she asked. "Your eyes bend around corners?"

Except for a narrow hospital bed, a small veneered table which held a white metal basin, and the lamp, the room was unfurnished. There were no chairs, pictures, or curtains. On the table was a radio.

"You're it," the old woman said, her palsied head always nodding. "Sometimes I look out a window. It was you back up in them scrubs. I thought it might be a dog or a fox."

Her hand lowered from the lamp and lay flopping in her lap. Her heavy flesh trembled under the black dress.

"I do have eyes," she said. "About everything else is gone, but us Ackers has always had eyes."

"Nobody's been in this room" he said.

"I been," she said. "Ain't it a pretty house? Billyboy, my son, he's hatched himself some fancy eggs. He's this minute up at a white clubhouse on the hill dancing under chandeliers and eating shrimp with a silver fork. You seen his swimming pool? He's the best yet, Billyboy is."

As she talked, she wheezed. Her breath sounded like distant tin whistles.

"And ain't Pam pretty?" she asked. "His childhood sweetheart. Almost as pretty as I was. There was a time men fought over me. Perce, the man I married, came to me with blood on him."

She never seemed to blink. Her shaking squeaked the cane wheelchair. He walked into the hall.

She started clapping and singing. The folded growth on her neck jostled her shoulder. Her quivering voice was as light as a girl's.

> Down by the willows
> Where the pure water flows,
> I been washed so clean
> That sin can't grow.

He walked back into the room. She sucked her lip and smiled.

"Where's the money?" he asked.

"Money?" she asked.

"And jewelry?" he asked.

"I don't know nothing about that," she said.

"You hear what she does with her jewelry box," he said.

"I don't listen," she said. "I got other noises in my head. My husband Perce was a dancing man. He was so strong he won money for lifting a mule off the ground, but he could dance a girl right onto a cloud. They all loved him. I can still hear that music."

Richard again walked into the hall. She kept talking.

"Perce used to make good money in the mines. Every summer we drove a Ford car to Atlantic City. One day the money stopped like somebody threw a switch. We lived on what we could grub. I gathered poke salad and dug ginseng. Perce cleared every squirrel and rabbit off that mountain. He shot robins. You ever eat a robin? They not so bad when your stomach's polishing your backbone. Even a young crow ain't bad. Clean sweet meat."

He walked to the wheelchair and held the flashlight like a club in front of her face.

"Where's the stuff?" he asked.

She drew her head away. For an instant it stilled. Then the wobbling returned, and she smiled. Her kinky hair quivered.

"You won't hurt me," she said.

"The hell I won't!" he said and raised the flashlight.

"You won't because you're afraid to touch me," she said.

She was smiling up at him, her bluish lips wavy, her head circling. She wore a faint cologne. Her face powder hadn't reached all the way into the deep creases of her skin. She lifted a hand toward him, the flesh ashy, the nails long, yellowed, and curved. He backed off and lowered the flashlight.

"See?" she said. "You're scared of me. Now me, I don't get afraid no more. My fear died with Perce under that old mountain. I washed his body, used laundry soap, and dressed him in his Sunday suit. My fear went into the grave with him."

She rubbed a hand over her eyes and face, and the leathery skin rasped.

"I seen terrible things," she said. "I was in a roadhouse where two men cut each other to pieces. Blood was all over the walls and tables. I seen union toughs tie a scab to a locust tree and beat him naked with planks tore off a shed. When I was a young widow living alone except for my Billyboy, a drunk black man climbed the mountain for me in the night. I shotgunned him coming through my bedroom window. Billyboy was bawling. I seen as much dying as living, so what do I got to be afraid of?"

Richard had been in the house too long. He left the room and walked the hallway to the carpeted steps. As he started down, headlights lashed and silvered the front windows. A car drove in the drive. The garage door whirred. He ran to the bottom of the steps but heard voices. He ran up the steps and back to the old woman's room.

"Probably had a little argument," she said. "Sometimes they have these little arguments."

"Don't talk!" he said, closing the door.

"I wouldn't do anything to hurt you," she whispered.

He stuck the flashlight into his hip pocket, held the knob with both hands, and cracked the door just enough to see a blur of the hall. The wife was shouting.

"You couldn't wait to get under her skirt, could you? You were out in the pro shop with her almost before I had my fur off!"

"You'd drive a cat into water," the man said.

Their shadows were swift on the walls of the stairwell. Richard closed the door and turned to the old woman, who watched. He walked around her wheelchair to raise both the window and the storm sash. Damp coldness and a wafer of snow blew into the room. Lights from windows checkered the ground. Under him wasn't grass, but the white metal table, flagstones, and empty flower pots. The plastic swimming pool cover snapped in the wind.

"You jump and you'll bust yourself," the old woman whispered.

He stripped the blanket off her bed and knotted the sheets. He tied one end to a leg of the bed. He fed the other end out the window.

"Them cheap sheets won't hold you," she whispered. "I'm not allowing you to cripple yourself. I swear I'll holler."

If she did, the man might become excited. Richard remembered the gun. He listened to the couple argue.

"Just a love fight," the old woman whispered. "In a little while they'll go to bed, and you can tiptoe right down through the house. They'll never know you was here. Now close the window before the end of my nose freezes off."

He almost hit her. His muscles gathered, and his fist tightened. She watched unafraid, her speckled green eyes the only part of her which didn't tremble. He drew in the sheets, unknotted them, and threw them on the bed. He closed the window. He crossed to the door, which he again opened a crack.

"You could've been nice to him!" the man shouted.

"I'm not letting that clammy wop politician give me a feel so you can sell concrete!" the wife shouted back.

"You let Basil Beard give you a feel, why not a wop politician?" the man asked.

"You're the one who's selling, you go to bed with him!" she shouted.

"Just a little show of temper," the old woman whispered. "They's a nice couple, handsome, Lettie a doll baby, only she don't like me to call her Lettie. That's a coal-camp name. She changed hers to Pam which she read in a magazine."

The couple argued. Shadows slashed the stairwell walls. Richard closed the door.

"Of course she shouldn't talk so mean to Billyboy," the old woman whispered. "Perce wouldn't tolerate that. I nagged him once in front of his friends, and it shamed him. When they left the house, he hit me so hard I had to hold to the icebox to stay on my feet. For about a week I thought the world had been knocked cockeyed."

Downstairs the voices quieted. Richard cracked the door. Somebody was coming up the steps. He shut the door.

"Get in the closet!" the old woman whispered.

He went in among dresses and gowns, not the old woman's, but cool silky material which was bright and perfumed. On the floor was a line of stylish pumps and clogs. His knees tumbled them. He pulled the closet door shut. His tools clinked. He was shaking and ready to bolt. He held the crowbar ready. The door to the room opened.

"What'd you tear up your bed for?" the man asked. "Don't I have enough trouble with the bitch?"

"Don't you worry, I'm going to fix my bed," the old woman said.

"I can do it fine from the chair."

"Looks like I could go out for a few minutes and not come in to find things torn up," the man said.

"Billyboy, you're tired and out of temper. I'll fix my bed. You go on and rest yourself."

"It sure looks like my women would try to help instead of working against me," the man said. "God knows I have enough on me without having to fight the women."

"You're just out of temper," the old woman said. "The liquor does it to you. Did it to your father."

"It's not the liquor," he said. "It's the damn load."

"I'm sorry I been a bother, and I think you ought to go rest some," she said.

"You think I can rest in there with the bitch?" he asked. "There's no rest anywhere in this house."

"Well I'm sorry, and you go on, 'cause I don't need nothing," the old woman said.

"Oh hell no, not a thing except the food you lick up, the clothes on your back, and the bed you wallow in and mess. I even had to pay the lawyer you sicced on me."

"Billyboy, you're just giving me things I gave you. They're my due."

"What's my due?" he asked. "What'd I break out of that damn black hollow and the coal grubbing and go to the university for? When have I had a minute's rest?"

"Don't help her!" the wife shouted. "Let her get in her own bed."

"I'm not helping her!" the man shouted.

"I'm not asking for nothing, Billyboy," the old woman said.

"You asked the damn lawyer," he said.

"It was the agency that done it, not me," the old woman said.

"Don't help her!" the wife shouted. "Let her do something herself."

"I'm not helping!" the man shouted.

"It's my due," the old woman said.

"Yeah and it's my dues to have to find the money to pay your dues," the man said. "Why aren't you in the bed? You don't need to burn my electricity to sit up here all night and think of ways to ruin my life."

He clicked off the light, walked out, and slammed the door. Richard waited. He heard distant voices. It was the television set. The old woman's wheelchair squeaked.

"Boy!" she called softly.

He opened the closet door. He couldn't see her in the darkness and shined his flashlight on her. Her head was bowed and bobbing. She straightened in the chair.

"It's liquor and his worry," she whispered. "Billyboy's having business troubles. Republicans in the statehouse naturally give the honey to their own swarm of bees."

Richard crossed to the door. Through it he heard a car wax commercial.

"Billyboy's out of temper at me too," she whispered. "He'll get over it, but a lawyer threatened him. Billyboy would've been happy to take care of me anyhow, but he didn't like that lawyer. It shamed him."

Through the door Richard heard sirens, shooting, and a clanging bell. He switched off the flashlight and cracked the door. One of the man's black shoes lay overturned on the green carpet of the hall.

"It's Lettie," the old woman whispered. "She's afraid people will find out we're coal camp. When her friends come, she pulls the blinds and locks me in the room. She won't let me eat at the table evenings. Why she'd turn to rain water and sink right into the ground if any of her new friends saw me."

Richard started to run out, but shadows slid across the bedroom wall. Quickly he closed the door.

"I know I'm a burden," the woman whispered. "What a lot of people wants is for me to drop into the grave, but it's my pride I won't. Us Ackers has always been gifted with long life. I'll sit here in the dark and not show myself, but I won't go to the grave till a team of angels' mules drags me. It's my pride."

"Sh-h-h," Richard said and again opened the door. Over the sound of television he heard the wife's voice.

"I won't do it!" she said. "I have to have a car!"

A reddish sheen flickered from their doorway. Richard stepped into the hall and hurried past the bedroom. The television splayed colors on the carpet and furniture. Wearing only undershorts, the man lay face down on the bed. Clothes were thrown about. The wife in a luminous pink slip and barefooted stood beside the bed folding hose and gesturing. Her blonde hair was unbound. Her painted face turned in fright.

"What?" she asked.

Richard ran down the steps to the front door. He got it unlocked, but the night chain jammed. There was commotion upstairs. He hacked at the chain with the crowbar. The old woman began to yell.

"Don't do nothing!" she shouted. "You all come to me!"

She gave him time. Screws of the night latch fractured wood. He yanked open the door and ran around the house and up the slope. Snow struck his face. Lights were switching on. He climbed to the ridge. The old woman's room was lighted. He ran into the gusty hollow where scrubs whipped his legs.

As he crossed the iron bridge, he tried to walk naturally. He'd left his brogans beside the laurel bush, and his feet were wet. He threw his tools and gloves into the black river. A white police cruiser sped past, its red light flashing and reflecting on slush. He used alleys and back lawns to reach the garage apartment. His mother was in bed. She raised herself to call his name.

He finally slept but woke during the night. It was still snowing. The horn of a coal tug sounded along the muffled river valley. His right hand was stretched up into darkness toward the hill as if there were something for him to touch.

Your Hand, Your Hand

After his swim Thursday afternoon in the satiny pool of the private hospital—the zinc-nosed, college-boy lifeguard made him paddle three lengths—Buzz walked into the brick building and past the nurses' station to his room on the second floor. The room had pale green carpeting, two comfortable armchairs, a writing table, a single bed, and a large, strongly screened window which looked down over mowed bluegrass to the James River of Virginia. Patients in colored bathrobes sat in slatted wooden chairs, their faces lifted to September sun.

Buzz showered and put on clean yellow pajamas which had been laid across his bed. He also had a clean red bathrobe and a pair of white washable slippers. As he adjusted the slippers to his feet, he was relieved that his hands were not bad at all. He had hardly any trouble tying the slippers.

His door opened, and Miss Ivers came in.

"Surprise for you," she said and smiled. She was in her middle twenties, a small brunette whose legs were quick and muscled in white stockings. When she walked, her hips pumped against starched cotton.

"Lib?" he asked, the word out before his mind had time to block it—as if all along he'd been expecting her to return from Connecticut.

"You come on," Miss Ivers said and held the door for him.

Buzz tied the belt of his bathrobe and walked past her. Her starched uniform crackled. She smelled of both cologne and antiseptic. She led him downstairs and out of the building into the late afternoon sunlight which slanted between branches of wan locust trees. Grass was spongy under his slippered feet.

"Am I—?" he asked, but he couldn't finish because he couldn't believe they would let him go so soon.

"Are you what?" Miss Ivers asked, smiling.

"Am I leaving?" he said and felt embarrassed.

"We'll see," she said and kept smiling, a smile no larger or smaller for him than for any other patient, though she'd once come to him in the night and laid her strong cool hand on his hot, moist brow.

They crossed under locust shade toward the Administration Building, a one-story brick-and-glass structure with a white screened-in porch. Around the base of the porch were drooping yellow flowers, and in front of the building was a fountain—water splashing from the mouth of a bronze dolphin held by a laughing boy with tangled hair.

In spite of himself Buzz hoped. He knew patients always went to the Administration Building before they were discharged. He looked toward the gravel parking lot, wanting to see Lib. Perhaps she and Dr. Bodine were having a conference, and she was explaining her willingness to take Buzz home, to open the house and clean out the dust.

Again Miss Ivers held doors for him. She stepped after him into a hallway lighted by fluorescent tubes. She led him to a room where a colored orderly in a white uniform worked at a counter across a doorway.

"Give Mr. Dyer his clothes and effects," she said.

The orderly walked among wooden racks until he found tags with Buzz's name on them. The clothes had been cleaned and covered by polyethylene bags.

"Is anyone here for me?" Buzz asked and looked up the corridor. His fingers trembled against his thighs.

"You get dressed," Miss Ivers said and opened the door of a white cubicle. She turned on a light. The cubicle had hooks for his clothes. She shut the door on him.

As he took off his pajamas and changed into his underwear, shirt, and checkered suit, his fingers fluttered. The suit was of good quality but shabby because of late he hadn't spent much on clothes. In fact he'd hardly been aware of what he had on his back as he found himself sitting dirty and unshaved in lawn chairs behind his house. The flower garden was weedy, and the grass grew high and ragged around him. He sat in the chairs and seemed to become a part of the wild vegetation—of the sweet peas and thistles growing up among bending lilies.

It had to be Lib, he thought. Only she would be able to work Dr. Bodine so quickly. Of course it could be Melton, Buzz's trustee at the bank who was again dipping into capital to pay bills—some hundred dollars a day plus medication—but Melton was unlikely because he'd arranged for Buzz to come to the hospital in the first place.

No, it was Lib, back from Connecticut and taking charge, she slim and tall, nervously impatient, still girlish at thirty-six, coltish, as she'd been the night after a junior cotillion when he first saw her. She was in the country club pool. She'd evidently sneaked outside, away from the St. Catherine's girls, and her clothes were tossed onto a metal chair. In the milky water her nakedness was a sort of bluish white. He stood gaping.

"Haven't you ever seen anybody in the buff before?" she asked. She swam unhurriedly into shadows. She ordered him to throw her a towel, and he didn't even know her name.

He opened the door of the white cubicle, half expecting to see her standing in the hospital corridor, dressed in something sporty, maybe bright slacks, sandals, and a white blouse, with a colored scarf around her light brown hair. She'd be smoking and have some gently sarcastic remark for him, as if they'd seen each other yesterday instead of it being almost two years since he came home to find her note propped against the clock. He was frantic and called all over the country until he found her at her sister's house in Palm

Beach. He talked to her half the night on the phone, both of them crying, he holding onto the banister with one hand and the telephone with the other, sick and sweating. He finally slid down, slowly, as if he were punctured and the air leaking out.

"We broke it, Buzz," Lib said, weeping. "There's no way to glue it back."

She was not in the hospital corridor. Miss Ivers was. She took Buzz's pajamas, slippers, and robe. She gave them to the orderly behind the counter who had Buzz's personal effects set out—wallet, silver penknife, change, reading glasses, cigarette lighter, and wristwatch. Miss Ivers helped strap on the watch.

"I wound it for you," she said, her young hands quick and sure.

"But who's here?" Buzz asked and looked up the bright corridor. The polished vinyl floor and metallic handrails reflected purling tube lights set in an acoustical ceiling.

"Come on," Miss Ivers said and nudged him along. He wanted to turn back and say some word of good-by to the orderly. He would have liked to say good-by to patients he knew—Tally, the investment banker with eyes full of terror, and Gibson, who'd been in the State Department and occasionally lifted invisible bugs off himself and shuddered. Buzz raised a hand to the orderly, a small gesture, and the orderly smiled.

"It's much sooner than I expected," Buzz said as he walked beside Miss Ivers.

"Is it?"

"I wonder whether you'd tell me who's here."

"Here?"

"Somebody must have come for me."

"We'll go down this way," she said.

They were at the elevator, and she pushed the ivory button set into the wall. Olive-colored doors slid open. He followed Miss Ivers on. The elevator lowered quietly.

He was really trembling. His knees bumped one another. His fingers danced at his sides. His toes shook in his shoes. He pictured Lib in Dr. Bodine's office. Buzz would kiss her, and they'd never mention the trouble. They'd go home, he'd unbutton her blouse, and they would be kind to each other.

"Is there anything else I have to do before I leave?" Buzz asked Miss Ivers.

"One or two formalities," she said.

"I expect Dr. Bodine will want to talk to me."

"I'm sure of it," she said.

The elevator stopped, and the doors opened smoothly. Miss Ivers walked off and led him along a white corridor to a dark door. She twisted the brass knob. He heard a faint music.

"Just go on in," she said, stepping back and holding the door for him.

"What's in there?" he asked.

"Nobody's going to bite you," she said.

He sidled into a sort of blue darkness, a hushed blue glow that illuminated wall drawings of cancan dancers, their ruffled skirts tossing. The music was a cocktail piano, the tones as soft as if they came from cotton. He turned back to the door, but Miss Ivers motioned him on.

"Keep going," she said.

"What am I supposed to do here?" he asked.

"They'll tell you," she said and pulled the door closed.

He stood in the blue glow. He recognized the tune on the piano—"They Can't Take That Away from Me." He heard laughter and glasses clinking. Frightened, he walked slowly, his shaky hands pushed in front of him. His feet were silent on the dark carpet. The piano became louder, and he heard talking. A woman giggled.

The blue passageway turned hard right, and he faced a room. He stopped breathing. A circular bar surrounded an island of bottles lined up before faceted mirrors. Golden light played on the bottles and mirrors. The effect was like a sunrise.

The same golden light spun slowly on walls and on murals of dancing senoritas. Below the dancers, in padded booths, couples sat, barely discernible in shadows—black silhouettes against gold. On a small stage at the front of the room a black man stroked piano keys. He sang in a whisper, "Oh no, they can't take that away from me."

Buzz looked again at the bar. Sitting on a stool was a young woman wearing a black cocktail dress. She had short dark hair, and her arms were bare and white. The black straps of her dress glittered on her white shoulders. Her legs were crossed, and she was smoking. She smiled, slipped off the stool, and walked toward him.

"Would you like to sit at the bar?" she asked, like a hostess, and he stared because she resembled one of the nurses he'd passed on the grounds. In the light he couldn't be sure.

"What is this?" he asked and rubbed a hand over his eyes and face.

"There's plenty of room," she said, smoking. Tiny gold earrings caught the light and reflected it against her cheeks.

"Am I crazy?" he asked. He would've laughed except he was scared. He peered at shadowy figures in the booths.

"You don't look crazy to me," she said and touched his arm to start him across the soft carpet to the bar. She positioned a leather stool for him.

"This can't be happening," he said. He tried to back away, but she caught his sleeve and tugged at him.

"You mean you don't want a drink?" she asked. She looked disappointed. She hooked a black heel over a stool rung and slid onto the seat.

A black man in a red jacket, white shirt, and red bowtie came from behind the island of bottles. For an instant Buzz thought him to be one of the orderlies, somebody Buzz had seen on the lawn or in the dining room. Golden braid on the red jacket curled around brass buttons.

"Yes, sir?" the bartender asked, leaning toward Buzz.

"I know I'm going crazy," Buzz said. He turned all the way around. The piano player hunched dreamily over the keys. Glasses clinked in booths.

"At least sit by a lonesome gal," the girl said and indicated the stool. She crossed her legs, and her nylons rasped. She smoothed her black dress, pushing her hands along her thighs. She patted the stool. "You don't object to sitting by me, do you?"

"I'm going to wake up," Buzz said. The bartender was still

waiting politely.

"If you're asleep, you may as well enjoy the dream," the girl said and again patted the stool.

Cautiously Buzz sat and brought his shaky feet up to the solid rungs. He stared at the island of bottles, all sorts of bottles, short and tall, skinny and chunky, long- and squat-necked. Colors blazed—red, yellow, sunbursts.

"What's your pleasure, sir?" the bartender asked. His groomed fingers rested on the edge of the bar.

"Well," Buzz said and laughed nervously. As his eyes swept the bottles, his stomach clenched like a fist. "I'll have to give this careful consideration."

"Harry makes a lovely Manhattan," the girl said.

"I think I'll have bourbon. As long as I'm dreaming, I'll have a double bourbon on the rocks. Wild Turkey on cubes."

The bartender backed away, and the girl smiled. Her eyes matched the blue dimness beyond the bar.

"Don't wake me yet," Buzz said. He peered at the girl, trying to see her in a starched uniform and place her as a nurse.

"You can feel this, can't you?" the girl asked and scratched the back of his hand with a sharp red fingernail.

"I can feel it," he said and took her hand. It was cool and smelled of perfumed soap.

"Then we're real," she said and drew her hand away to reach for her drink.

"But how?" he asked, looking around the room at the booths and the piano player. Buzz raised his eyes, thinking of the hospital and everybody above ground.

"Don't worry about that now," the girl said. "The secret of happiness is not to worry about now."

The bartender brought the drink on a silver tray. He set the bourbon in front of Buzz. Buzz reached for his wallet, but the bartender shook his head.

"It's been taken care of," he said.

"By whom?" Buzz asked. He again had the impression the bartender was an orderly.

"There you go," the girl said. "Just count your blessings."

Buzz's tongue touched his lip, and he stared at the drink. The bourbon was in an Old Fashioned glass which had a white knit skirt. The light from the island of bottles made the liquor appear pure and golden. He moved a trembling hand toward the glass but drew back.

"What's the matter?" the girl asked. She and the bartender were watching.

"It doesn't make sense," Buzz said. He leaned away from the drink. "This is the reason—"

He stopped. He didn't want to tell the girl—as he'd had to tell Dr. Bodine—about those last days when he roamed the rooms of his empty house or circled unsteadily about his thistle-grown garden, sometimes tripping and lying in the long grass or becoming so weak he had to crawl to the house. He got bombed in his bathtub and couldn't climb out. Like a man drowning, he shouted until neighbors sent the police.

"You were saying?" the girl asked.

"Nothing of consequence," Buzz told her and stared at the drink. His hands twitched. He thought of Lib and how they'd once carried a bottle of French champagne out in a black innertube to float down the Rappahannock. Her pretty legs were wet and brown against his. They both became addled by the sun and wine and spun slowly into the bay. She kissed his neck and fell asleep with her face against his chest. He nodded into her fragrant hair. The Coast Guard picked them up.

"Your ice is melting," the girl said. The bartender had backed off into shadows.

Again Buzz moved a hand toward the drink as if the glass might try to escape or strike at him. His fingers were shaking terribly. He slid them along the bar and stopped them just short of the base of the glass.

"What's the matter?" the girl asked.

"This is still the hospital," he said.

"Forget the hospital," she said, impatient.

"I can't when I know it's upstairs."

"When you go home you're going to forget the hospital, aren't you?" the girl asked. "Why make a big deal out of it?"

Her words sounded his way of life. He'd always pushed aside problems to seize the moment. He and Lib both had, though Lib was not as good at it as he was. Her conscience occasionally bothered her. Now and then she felt compelled to put things in order. She'd straighten the house and urge him to see about having his blood pressure checked or to go to the trust department of the bank to talk to Melton about finances.

"I though Lib might be here," he said. He glanced at the girl, hoping her expression might tell him something.

"Who?" the girl asked.

"My wife. At least she was my wife. She married a college professor who teaches chemistry in Connecticut. She took my daughter."

The girl said nothing. Her red upper lip was wet with drink, and she cleaned the lip delicately with the tip of her pink tongue.

"I thought maybe she had something to do with this," Buzz said. He raised a hand to indicate the room. "I thought perhaps she and Dr. Bodine were having a little talk and arranged things."

"Anything's possible," the girl said. "You're letting Harry's lovely bourbon evaporate."

Buzz's fingers, like exploring antennae, patted the glass softly. He was frightened by the swoop of darkness he knew lay at the bottom of the drink. This bar had to be part of a hospital routine—if he weren't dreaming—possibly part of a program to condition patients to withstand liquor. He sensed he should be careful, that he was being manipulated.

"If you don't mind, I'll wait a minute or two longer," he said.

"Why should I mind?" she asked and shrugged.

The piano player changed tunes. His hands were limp on the keys. He hummed, "I've Got You under My Skin."

"I'd like to think it's Lib," Buzz said. "I'd like to think she and Puss are waiting for me."

"Puss?"

"My daughter. She's fourteen."

"Well," the girl said and lit a cigarette with a hand that was marvelously steady.

"She's a fine daughter, but she takes her mother's side," Buzz said. "Which I shouldn't blame her for."

He thought of the night he and Lib battled, when they ranged over the house shouting and breaking furniture. He hit her with his fist, and she stumbled weeping among chairs, holding her face. Then they both looked to the steps where Puss stood, pale and terrified, clutching a toy animal and holding her nightgown up close to her throat.

"You crying?" the girl at the bar asked, peering at him.

"Just something in my eye," he said and wiped at his face.

"I thought for a minute you were crying," the girl said.

"No," he said. He pulled out his handkerchief. The girl looked away as he dabbed at his eyes.

"You all right now?" she asked after a moment.

"I'm fine," he said and put away his handkerchief. He blinked against mist. "I hope someday my daughter will understand."

"Understand what?" the girl asked and sipped her drink.

"That things go wrong. It's nobody's fault."

"You worry too much," the girl said.

"Just lately. I've been feeling my age. I found myself thinking about—" He stopped.

"About what?" the girl asked.

"About death," he said and felt ashamed.

"Ugh!" the girl said and made a face. He stared at her. He believed she was a nurse he'd passed in the Craft Shop.

"I remember you now," he said, leaning toward her. "You had a handful of yellow yarn."

"Ho-hum," she said.

"In the Craft Shop," he said. "You were helping the weavers."

"Was I really?" she asked and yawned. She had powder along her pretty young throat. "I thought you were going to be a sport."

Somebody laughed in a booth. He looked at the shadowy couples. The piano player's fingers moved languidly in "What Is This Thing Called Love?"

"Dr. Bodine has to know this place is here," Buzz said. Dr. Bodine was a studious young man with a face like a washed egg.

"You are turning into a bug," the girl said. She wrinkled her nose. "And I heard you were a swinger."

"Look at the gray in my hair," he said and touched it at the temple.

"You're not that old," she said. "Try your drink."

"I used to swing," Buzz said. He thought of Lib and him after his graduation from the university. They went up into mountains around Charlottesville, he driving recklessly along a fire trail. Lib carried a thermos full of martinis. She was dressed in pink tulle and pink velvety slippers. He stopped his convertible, and she danced ahead of him in the clean early morning. She kicked off her slippers and ran through the forest. He caught her and hung her clothes from a blooming dogwood—her slip, stockings, girdle. Her pink gown belled with the breeze.

"It's hard to believe," the girl said. She looked at his drink.

"Lib and I tried to go to all the parties," he said. At Christmas the big gilt mirror over the hall table was rimmed with invitations—at least it was until the Hamilton ball when Buzz poured a drink down the back of his blond hostess. She was wearing a red dress slashed in a great V almost to her rump, and it was such a natural place to empty a glass. She shrieked and wept. After that there weren't so many invitations, and Lib suggested they cut down the drinking.

"We like it too much," Lib said. "We get too happy."

"How can you get too happy?" he asked her. At the very moment he had his hands on a bottle of Old Crow.

Lib stopped on him. He'd come home in the afternoons to find her working in the garden, her long aristocratic legs bent under her as she troweled the soil, her white blouse pulled tightly over her breasts, her face shaded by a floppy sunhat. No drinks would be waiting moistly on the garden table. He would have to walk to the kitchen for the things, and she'd look the other way.

"You trying to make me feel guilty?" he asked her.

"I just don't care for one, thanks," she said. She was almost prim.

"I don't like to drink alone," he said, but he drank to drunkenness to punish her. She, of course, couldn't stay off long, and one night at the club when she listed on her high heels, she went out onto a dark balcony with Jerry Jackson. Buzz tried to hit Jerry, who was sober and strong and knocked Buzz down concrete steps. Lib screamed and ran to him. She put Buzz's bloody head in her lap and dabbed at his wounds with the slick, cool skirt of her blue dress. A crowd, some of the people holding glasses, gathered to watch. Lib wept. "Are you in pain?" she asked and kissed him. She wailed, "Oh Lord I'm sorry!"

The black waiter took shape in front of Buzz. The braid on his red jacket reflected golden lights. He stood solicitously, his head inclined.

"Something wrong with your drink?" he asked. His voice was whispery, confidential.

"I know you're one of the orderlies," Buzz said, blinking to focus.

"If you don't like the drink, I'll take it back," the bartender said. "No charge."

"He hasn't even tasted it," the girl said. She hummed to the piano music—"This Love of Mine." The hum came not from her throat but from deep within her body.

"I'll fix you another," the bartender said and reached for the glass.

"No," Buzz said. "But thanks."

The bartender withdrew his hand and drifted back into shadows. Buzz listened to the piano. Black fingers seeemed hardly to touch the keys.

"Lib and I used to go to a bar like this," Buzz said. He tried to think of the bar's name. It was The Paradise.

"Did you?" the girl asked. She jiggled her foot.

"In Florida when I was in the Air Force. I'd meet her before supper, and we'd have a couple of drinks and listen to the piano. Some of the same tunes."

"Personally I like my music to jive," the girl said. She covered her mouth with her fingers.

"We played a lot of golf," Buzz said. "I usually got beat."

"Your wife beat you?"

"Lib," he said and nodded. "She was a beautiful golfer—long

and smooth. She could always beat me."

"I don't care much for golf," the girl said.

"I don't think she plays anymore. She has her professor up in Connecticut."

"I think I'm going to leave," the girl said. She uncrossed her legs and shifted her weight on the stool.

"Please don't," Buzz said. He didn't want to be alone, at least until he knew for sure whether or not Lib was here.

"Well drink your drink," the girl said.

"I'm going to," he told her. His shaky fingers again slid toward the glass. "You know when I first came here I couldn't sleep. I tried counting sheep, and they turned into martinis. Clear, moist martinis jumping the fence. You ever heard of that?"

"I wish you'd stop trembling," the girl said. "You're trembling all over."

"I can tell you I'm aware of it."

"You really are trembling everywhere. Look at your knees."

He looked at his knees and saw them flapping the fabric of his pants.

"I can't seem to help it," he said.

"Well a drink would help," she said. She cupped her young hands around his and fitted his fingers to his glass.

"I'm certain you're right," he said, very much afraid. "But you see I've had this little problem with drink. Lib and I began to have this little problem, and to be perfectly frank it's one of the reasons she went up to Connecticut and I came here."

"What harm can one drink do?" the girl asked. With her hands she encouraged him to lift the glass.

"You really think it's all right?" Buzz asked. He raised the glass, but he was shaking so badly that the bourbon spilled. He had to set the glass down quickly.

"Some mess," the girl said and wiped his hands with a cocktail napkin. The bartender came holding a towel.

"I'll be all right in a second," Buzz said and tried to laugh. They were drying him off. "It's crazy the way I'm shaking. I used to be very co-ordinated. In fact I was a first-class tennis player. Lib could always beat me at golf, but I was first rate at tennis and twice won the club trophy. If I'd won the third year, I'd have been allowed to keep the silver cup."

"I saw your picture in the paper," the girl said and crumpled the cocktail napkin. The bartender took it from her. "When I was younger."

"I had pictures in the paper all right. I played an exhibition at the Country Club of Virginia with Pancho Segura. It was just an exhibition, but he told me I played very solid tennis."

"Let me help you with your glass," the girl said. Again she cupped her hands around his—confident white hands with red nails. Her grip was strong and contained his shaking. The glass rose. He had an impulse to kiss her fingers.

"Well," he said, his lips close to the drink, pecking at it. Bourbon fragance expanded through his nose and head. "God bless the ladies."

He ducked his mouth to the glass and closed his eyes. The bourbon passed over his tongue and sank into his throat. He sipped a second time. He waited for warmth and the flowing into softness.

Instead his mouth burned. He felt a pump of nausea. The girl released him and leaned quickly away. His glass pitched wildly. He put his mouth on it, and the rim clinked against his teeth. The glass jerked as if it had life. He got it down to the counter where it thumped and the bourbon sloshed out.

The girl was off her stool. She gestured to somebody across the room. The bartender came from shadows. The piano player lifted his hands from the keys and stood, but the music didn't stop. Even as the player hurried across the room, the piano kept on.

Suddenly sick, Buzz would have fallen from his stool had not the girl and bartender caught him. His head bumped the counter. His mouth was on fire, and his stomach heaved. He was sweating and sucking for air. The piano player helped hold him. Orderlies in white uniforms were coming from shadowed booths. The starched uniforms of nurses crackled. Through his gagging, Buzz heard the piano playing "Love for Sale."

They caught him by his arms and half-carried, half-dragged him across the room and through a door. He was in a white-tiled lavatory. They held him over a medical sink just as hot vomit shot up through his mouth and nose. He couldn't stop retching. He choked and humped. His legs gave under him, but orderlies and nurses held him so that he stayed over the sink.

He almost fainted. A pretty hand reached into his graying hair and pulled back his head so that he had to see himself in the mirror. He stared at his sweating, agonized face. He looked as if he'd been beaten. Behind him he glimpsed the girl talking to Dr. Bodine. Dr. Bodine wore a white smock and made notes on a chart. He nodded as he listened to the girl. He appeared studious and calm.

Buzz bent to the sink. Wave after wave of nausea racked him. He was strangling and clawed, but they held him at the sink. He became limp, his arms and legs boneless. He was spinning and sinking. Finally they allowed him to collapse.

"Clean him and take him to his room," Dr. Bodine said matter-of-factly. He continued to make notes.

"And hurry," the girl said. She arranged her hair in front of the mirror. "We have another one."

They washed Buzz with a wet towel and carried him out. Golden light touched his weeping eyes. He had a last murky impression of the girl arranging herself on her stool at the bar. She smoothed her dark cocktail dress over her thighs.

The piano still played, though no one sat at it. The tune sounded distantly familiar, but in the bright light of the antiseptic corridor Buzz could not remember the name of the song.

Amazing Grace

The way we knew was that Nana, my grandmother, stopped making bread and instead of running the kitchen like a drill sergeant she walked out into the front yard and sat on a bench under the Indian cigar-tree.

"Maybe she's tired," my father said when he and I came in from changing the tire on the John Deere. "There's times I'd like to sit under that tree."

"That's not it," my mother said and slapped at me for reaching to get a hot corn-dodger from the stove.

My mother had to drive to the store to buy us bread. None of us remembered how sorry store-boughten tasted because Nana baked three times a week ever since I could remember—biscuits, rolls, and loaves, some of the loaves salt-rising bread which smelled up the house, and she had a cool dusky pantry with wooden shelves where she set her dough and bread, covering them with clean white cloths. Though there was a GE electric stove in the kitchen now, she still liked the old wood-burning Kalamazoo for her baking, or had until she walked out to sit under the Indian cigar-tree.

She sat and looked past the plank fence to the meadow and past the meadow to the barbed-wire fence at the road. Beyond the road the valley sloped up to a ridge, and on the other side of that ridge was Virginia, but here in the valley it was West Virginia, not the coal-mining part, but farming. The grassy hills had outcroppings of limestone, and sometimes it was hard to see the difference between the limestone and sheep grazing the slopes.

"It's Henry," my mother said to my father on Wednesday night after Nana went to bed. My mother and father were sitting in the kitchen, at the metal table that had paper towels for mats, their arms on the table, sitting not to eat or drink but to talk. My father was tall, which was unusual for us Sharps, who ran to heft, yet he had their blond hair and heaviness of jaw, like me. My mother, a Henson, was a small woman, though strong, and her hair and eyes were dark brown.

"What about Henry?" my father asked.

"He's not been to the river," my mother said. "None of his has."

My daddy's two sisters, Aunt Henrietta and Aunt Cornelia, were both older than him. They and their husbands, Albert and Asa, came the next night to the kitchen, again after Nana was in bed. It was agreed my father should speak to Henry in person since that would be more effective than just a letter or a phone call. Early Friday Daddy put on his gray suit and drove the Ford pickup to Pittsburgh.

The night he came back I was scrubbing my hair. Every Saturday night I had to wash my hair, and my mother inspected it, parted the hair to look at my scalp the way a person would search for a dime lost in the grass.

"They own a house out of town now," my father said. "Place called Sewickley, kind of in the country."

"Smoke and grit?" my mother asked.

"Not yesterday and today when I left, though Henry never minded smoke and grit," my father said. "Henry always claims smoke and grit shakes off money. You can live clean and pure in the desert where the air's perfect, Henry says, but that's all you got except sand. Where people do honest work, there's going to be some smoke and grit, Henry says."

"Dale Blue still have the same color hair?" my mother asked about Henry's wife.

"That's enough," my father said.

Uncle Henry was the member of the family who'd left. He first played football for West Virginia University, right tackle, and afterwards he became a mining engineer. His job took him to the southwest part of the state near Kentucky, and while he was driving a shaft into a seam of bituminous coal a steel company bought the seam, and he found himself in the steel business. Now he had an office in Pittsburgh overlooking the Monongahela River and barges carrying his money.

"That's not coal in those barges," he told me when he came back to the farm and showed snapshots. "Those are black lumps of money being shoved to my bank."

That's the way I thought of him, sitting up high in his shiny office watching the tugs nose his money to the bank. I guess the bank had a rear door on the river to take the money through.

During the summer Nana sat under the Indian cigar-tree. One afternoon she lifted her chin, and I saw the car glint a long ways off. The road was paved, but the speed of the car still raised tan dust along both shoulders. The horn started honking. It had to be.

"It's him!" I shouted, running to Nana. "It's Uncle Henry!"

"Drives too fast," she said.

I'd seen pictures of Nana when she was a girl in high school, and she'd been thin, like my daddy, and smiling, her head lowered, her dark hair parted in the middle and pulled back, her eyes raised, her feet set a little pigeon-toed. It'd been graduation time, and she'd worn a white dress and black slippers.

Over the years she'd grown shorter and thicker, not fat because she'd never stayed still long enough to gather fat, but stout the way an oak tree is stout. When I kissed her before she went to bed, I felt the strength in her. She was no puny old woman. Her forearm was as hard as my father's. I'd seen her hit a mule so hard with a hoe handle that he was cross-eyed for ten minutes.

I climbed the plank fence, ran across the meadow, and jumped the ditch to open the gate for Uncle Henry. Naturally he came in his big car. He knew I'd be disappointed if he didn't. One of the things he'd do on visits was to take me in his car and run her up to about a hundred. This time it was a gunmetal Cadillac with white sidewalls and tinted windows.

Dale Blue, his wife, was in front beside him. Like my mother would, the first thing I did was look at her hair, yellowish now, though I'd seen it both black and platinum, sometimes short, sometimes long, now piled on top of her head in a twist. It reminded me of custard on a cone at the Tastee Freeze.

She was the prettiest woman I'd ever seen. We lived in the country, but we had TV, and I'd drive in the truck with Daddy to the livestock market in Lewisburg, so I'd seen some pretty women, but she was the best yet, always licked to a gloss, her jewelry glittering, her clothes bright and fresh, herself sweet-smelling. The last time she was on the farm I walked into the bathroom while she was drying and stepping from the tub, and I saw one of her creamy bosoms. I get hot in the face even thinking about it.

After opening and shutting the gate, I rode in with them. Dale Blue gave me a wet, perfumed kiss. Uncle Henry shook hands and roughed my hair. In the back seat was Dawson, their son and my cousin. He was my age. Though built low and square like the Sharps, he had red hair. As soon as his parents weren't looking, he frogged me on the arm. That frog jumped out at least three inches.

"Oh aw!" I said.

"What's that, hon?" Dale Blue asked, turning and smiling.

"Just clearing my throat," I said.

"Got him a frog in it," Dawson said.

Uncle Henry drove to the house. He didn't wait for Dale Blue or Dawson but was out of the car and vaulting the plank fence before they opened a door. He kissed Nana, hugged her, and knelt on the ground beside her, not caring about grass stain on his peach slacks.

"How come you sitting out here and not fixing me an angel food?" Uncle Henry asked. "You always fix me my angel food cake when I come."

"You going to the river before I die?" Nana asked.

"What, you die? Listen, Momma, I don't want any talk of dying around here, and I been wetted anyhow. I'm a bonafide deacon in the church. I have my own pew every Sunday, and I bought a big window showing Jesus with the twelve."

"You weren't wetted in our river," Nana said.

Dale Blue and Dawson had walked through the gate, and my mother was coming from the porch. My father drove his tractor toward the house. As soon as Uncle Henry was in the county, things happened. The summer air stirred, and our water ran cooler. We touched each other and laughed. No wonder the rich people in Pittsburgh liked him.

"And look here, Momma, here's Dale Blue and little Dawson," Uncle Henry said. "They all want to kiss you."

As she leaned to Nana, one of Dale Blue's diamond earrings got tangled in Nana's white hair. For a minute Dale Blue and Uncle Henry were laughing and calling out as they unsnagged the earring, but Nana wasn't laughing. She stared at Dale Blue and Dawson as if they'd stolen the church.

"None's been to the river," Nana said.

"Ah come on, Momma, forget the river a second, will you?" Uncle Henry said. He ran and jumped the plank fence to reach his Caddy. In the trunk he had presents for everybody. I got me a baseball mitt. My mother was handed a five-pound can of peanut brittle, and Daddy shouldered a big net sack of Florida grapefruits.

For Nana Uncle Henry had a clock, a grandfather clock which he and my daddy lugged in pieces across the grass and put together under the Indian cigar-tree. They leveled it and hooked on golden weights shaped like pine cones. The brass pendulum swung into a shaft of sunshine. When the clock ticked and gonged, the cows stopped grazing and lifted their heads. Two crows spiraled cawing from the corn.

"Eight days," Uncle Henry explained to Nana. "Eight whole days and you don't have to pull the chains to wind her."

Nana eyed the clock. She had an oval face, and her hair was thin, wispy cotton. She adjusted her glasses to peer at the clock. Then she turned away.

"But don't you like it?" Dale Blue asked. "Henry went to lots of trouble to bring it."

"All that clock tells me is my days are running out, and nobody's been to the river," Nana said.

She wouldn't look at the clock again. The men carried it into the hall to set it up a second time, but she went to bed without glancing at it. Uncle Henry and Dale Blue came to the kitchen where they sat around the table with my mother and daddy as well as Aunt Henrietta and Aunt Cornelia and their husbands Albert and Asa.

"She's sure low," Aunt Cornelia said while she poured iced tea from a glass pitcher, her arms brown from helping Uncle Asa in the hayfields. "I've not seen her this far down since lightning hit the heifers."

"Spoiled is what she is," Dale Blue said.

Boy, eyes bugged at Dale Blue as if she was a snake on a rock. She was in the family but not of it. She colored, touched her frozen-custard hair, and shrugged.

"Honey, maybe you better let me do the talking here," Uncle Henry said.

"But she's pouting like a child," Dale Blue said.

"All the work she's done for this family she's got a right to pout until Moses makes sauerkraut out of little sour apples in December," Aunt Henrietta said.

Dale Blue kind of sniffed, crossed her arms, and jiggled a pretty foot in a black-and-white slipper. From time to time while the others talked she'd raise her nose as if she wasn't sure she should be breathing the same air as the rest of us. She came from West Virginia too, from Beckley, but she didn't tell anybody if she could help it.

"Give me another day anyhow," Uncle Henry said, standing. "Maybe I can fun her up tomorrow."

"I know you're tired," my mother said. "The spare room's ready."

"Oh, well, we won't be needing the spare room, thanks," Dale Blue said. "Henry made us a reservation over at White Sulphur. Allows him to combine business with pleasure. The railroad men are having a convention."

Nobody said anything, first because they couldn't imagine a member of the family not staying at the farm and second because no one in our family had ever slept at the resort before—a white hotel covering acres and acres where they had a private airport, golf courses,

stables, and foreign servants who wore red jackets. To us in the
county the resort and grounds were like another country.

"I don't know whether you ought to do that, Henry," my father
said. "Momma might not understand."

"Blame me," Dale Blue said. "I've signed up for a bath."

"You can use the tub here," I said and thought of the time I'd
seen her creamy bosom fall over the lilac towel. I again got hot in the
face.

"Sh-h-h," my mother said to me, and Dawson snickered.

"What difference does it make except cause you all less trouble?"
Dale Blue asked. "Henry and Dawson will come back tomorrow and
spend the day."

She led them out to the car. We watched the Caddy's red taillights
in the darkness. My mother made me go up to bed, but I sneaked
down to hear them talking in the kitchen.

"Henry's changed," Aunt Henrietta said and sighed.

"It's not Henry," Aunt Cornelia said. "Nothing's wrong with
Henry."

"I wonder Dale Blue don't make him wear a bib at the table," my
daddy said.

I sank to sleep hearing the ticking and gonging of the grandfather
clock downstairs, and then I woke because I wasn't hearing it. I
peeked over the railing. Nana was at the clock. She held her
flashlight, and her hand had stilled the pendulum. She shuffled to
her bedroom.

"Can't sleep with all that clanging," she said.

The next morning I was mowing as soon as the sun dried the
orchard grass. I drove the small tractor, the Ford, running her in
second gear and keeping the swaths neat as the clattering blade
felled the grass. My father drove the big tractor, the John Deere, and
was pulling the bailer over windrows in a seven-acre field we'd cut
three days earlier. My uncles loaded bales on the wagon.

When Uncle Henry came, he too threw bales on the wagon. He
showed off his strength by tossing the bales like basketballs. He
laughed and joked with his brothers. He wasn't dressed for work but
wore a red shirt, apricot pants, and what he called shag chukkas,

which my daddy asked him to spell. Uncle Henry worked until he was sweat shiny.

He tried everything to cheer up Nana. He tuned the banjo, his old one from the hall closet, and sang "Rye Whiskey," "The Possum's Lament," and "The Coal Miner's Daughter." He stomped as he played, and later, sitting on the bench beside Nana, he told her stories about Pittsburgh and his new house which had doors that opened and closed when he pushed buttons. It had a sauna and a putting green.

"That house'll do everything for you except pick your teeth," he said.

"Will it bake bread?" I asked.

"Sh-h-h," my mother said.

Nana listened and watched. She kept her bluish-gray eyes on him every second, but she never smiled or put out her hand to him, though she loved him so much she'd set his picture on the center of the mantel in her bedroom. She had other pictures, but his was the place of honor, and she sometimes draped a rose or shasta daisy over the frame.

We ate lunch on the grass around the Indian cigar-tree, a picnic in the yard for all the hands—cold chicken, melons, and lemonade. Nana swallowed a bite or two, but not as if she enjoyed it. Mostly she nibbled and looked at the sheep on the sunny slope. She seemed to forget she was eating.

That afternoon Preacher Arbogast came. He drove a Chevy which he parked beside Uncle Henry's Caddy. Preacher Arbogast was a small pop-eyed man always washed to a waxy finish. When he walked, he did it like a person measuring every step. He shook hands around. There was chicken for him, but he wouldn't sit on the grass to eat it the way the rest of the men did. He let my daddy bring him a chair from the house.

"I was hoping to meet your wife this time, Henry," Preacher Arbogast said.

"She's in the bathtub all day," I said.

"Sh-h-h," my mother said, and Dawson again snickered.

After the picnic it was time to go back to haying. Nana, Uncle

Henry, and Preacher Arbogast stayed in the yard. I was now driving Uncle Asa's International and pulling the wagon. Dawson rode behind me on the drawbar. He wanted to steer.

"If a hick-freak like you can do it, anybody can," he said.

"Everybody in Pennsylvania got mouths as big as yours?" I asked.

He punched me in the ribs. I almost fell off the seat. My daddy saw us and hollered. Dawson jumped from the drawbar and walked to Daddy who listened to him. Daddy waved to stop me, came over to the tractor, and told me to teach Dawson to drive.

The thing that made me maddest was that after a few minutes Dawson drove the International almost as good as I could, that and the fact he got to sit up there in his new jeans and act like a king while I had to throw bales on the wagon. Those bales weighed fifty or sixty pounds. I was strong for my age, eleven, but it was man's work, and the next time we unloaded at the barn, I snuck to the house to see if I could find some of that picnic lemonade.

Nana, Preacher Arbogast, and Uncle Henry were still in the yard. I tiptoed through the front bedroom to listen at a window screen that flies buzzed around and bumped against.

"But, Momma, I got here an affidavit," Uncle Henry said. "It's signed and sworn to by my pastor in Sewickley. It's duly notarized. It proves I'm a baptized member of the church."

"You've not been baptized like a Sharp in our river," Nana said.

"But it's not required," Uncle Henry said. "Ask the Reverend Arbogast here about it, and he'll tell you I'm genuinely saved."

"Technically I have to agree," Preacher Arbogast said.

"What do you mean 'technically'?" Uncle Henry asked, and he was angry.

"Outside the denomination you've been," Preacher Arbogast said. "We don't know for sure what they're doing up in Pennsylvania."

"You telling me only you and the Greenbrier River Baptists around here can save me?" Uncle Henry asked, flapping his arms.

"All the Sharps has been to our river," Nana said. "You escaped because you were a sickly boy, and for a time we went without a

preacher. Then you slipped away from the county before anybody
remembered you'd not been in the river."

It's all I was able to hear. My mother came tiptoeing into the same
bedroom. She almost jumped out of her shoes when she pulled back
the curtain and saw me standing there looking at her. She yelped
and chased me off by shoving me on the back. I went, but I knew she
stayed and listened.

In the hayfield Dawson was wheeling around on the International.
My daddy stared at me and spat because I'd been gone. I again
threw bales on the wagon. Each time I lifted I grunted, and sweat
stung my eyes. Chaff made me sneeze. Dawson was driving the
tractor so fast I had to hurry with the bales. I fell, but he didn't wait.
He grinned at me.

When we finally got the field cleared and the bales stacked in the
barn, I lay down in the shade of a sycamore tree. I rested and wondered if Uncly Henry was going to be too worried to take me for a fast
ride in the gunmetal Caddy. Dawson walked by. He was still clean in
his T-shirt, pressed jeans, and white tennis shoes.

"What's the matter, Cousin Willie Hick-freak?" he asked.

"You going to make me get up out of this shade to whip you?" I
asked.

"You'd commit suicide just because I called you Willie Hick-
freak?" he asked. "Your name's Willie, isn't it, and you got to
admit you're a hick. At least that's what my momma says. Tell
me this: you ever been on a jet plane or an escalator?"

"No," I admitted.

"You ever eaten in a French restaurant or swum in an Olympic-
size pool?"

"No," I said.

"You ever seen the ocean?" he asked.

"No," I said.

"Then how can you claim you're not a hick-freak?" he asked.

"This is how," I said. I stood and punched him in the mouth.

He came back at me. He might be a city boy, but he was strong
like Uncle Henry and knew more about boxing than I did. He was
hitting me two or three times for every one I got him. I had to rush

him, trip him, and close the scissors on him. I also put the strangle-
hold on him. He was gasping in the grass.

"Tell me how sorry you are," I said.

"Sorry you're a hick-freak," he said.

I tightened up. He flopped around and became sick. I let go fast.
My nose was bleeding. I crawled away, lay on my back, and looked
at the yellowish sky.

"You don't fight fair," Dawson said, his head hung like a
whipped dog. "We were supposed to be boxing."

"You want to fight about what we were supposed to be doing?" I
asked.

"At my school you don't rassle and box at the same time," he
said.

"At your school the boys probably wear their hair like girls too," I
said.

"Yeah, some of them do," he said. "And I've been to a stylist."

He touched his hair like a girl would, and that got me laughing.
He started laughing. My nose had stopped bleeding. We walked to
the barn to wash ourselves at the spigot. We bowed our heads under
the water and blew into it. As to the bruise on my cheek, I told my
mother I'd slipped against the hay wagon. She glanced at Dawson
and would've questioned him about his torn T-shirt except she was
too excited with news of Uncle Henry.

"He's going to do it," she told my daddy. "Him and Dale Blue
and little Dawson."

"Little Dawson," I snickered.

"Has Dale Blue been told yet?" my daddy asked.

"Tonight," my mother said. "Give thanks."

"She ought to be clean enough," I said. "All day in a bath."

Dawson kicked me in the leg. Nobody saw him. I hopped around
and hollered.

"Sh-h-h," my mother said.

Next morning when I woke, I heard a sound, something more
than the birds, the cattle, and the creaking of the tin roof heating
under the sun. I walked to the hallway. My mother and daddy were
already standing there, she wearing her white nightgown, Daddy in

his undershorts. They were smiling, and I smiled too because down-stairs Nana was humming a hymn in her bedroom.

Still everybody was nervous Uncle Henry wouldn't be able to per-suade Dale Blue. We watched the road from White Sulphur. Daddy looked at his watch. Uncle Asa spat tobacco juice into the gerani-ums, and Aunt Cornelia fussed at him for it.

When the Caddy came, it raised a whirling rooster-tail of dust. I ran to the gate. Dale Blue was sitting in the car with Uncle Henry and Dawson. Nana had walked out onto the porch. Uncle Henry hurried to her and hugged her.

"It's okay, Momma," he said. "Tell that old river to get itself set because a bunch of sharp Sharps is coming."

Nana held onto him and laughed. I saw how lively and pretty she must've been as a girl. Dale Blue wore a pink scarf and a pink pantsuit. Though Nana didn't like women in breeches, she kept her-self from complaining and even offered her face to Dale Blue for a kiss. Dawson, while nobody was watching, tried to frog me. I was ready and elbowed him in the stomach. He moved around bent over. Uncle Asa drove off in his pickup to see if Preacher Arbogast could do the baptizing that afternoon.

"I don't understand how Henry swung it," Daddy whispered to my mother. "Dale Blue's acting almost pleased about going to the water."

I found out about that. Dawson and I ran to the barn to check the tractors and throw clods at the Hereford bull in the lot. We also punched each other a couple of times. Dawson was excited about the river.

"Will they let me swim?" he asked. "I never swam in anything except an Olympic-size pool and the ocean."

"No, you poor city-freak, Preacher Arbogast won't let you swim," I said. "He'll dunk you three times, but maybe you and me can slip back afterwards."

"If Momma doesn't get too worried about her hair," Dawson said. "I wish they didn't have to wet that."

"They do unless she can take it off first," I said.

"Well she shouldn't holler too loud since Dad's promised her a green Mercedes and a trip to Italy," Dawson said.

We ate lunch on the lawn. Daddy and my uncles carried out tables, and my mother and aunts covered them with Nana's linen cloths. Family arrived not only from Pocahontas County, but also from the other side of the mountain. They were served ham, snaps, deviled eggs, and seven kinds of pie people brought with them, including brown sugar, sweet potato, and lemon chess. Dawson and I gorged until we couldn't breathe except through our mouths. We were too bloated to punch each other. We stretched out on the grass and let flies walk over us.

"But what does one wear to the river?" Dale Blue asked, lifting her palms. "I simply don't have a thing with me."

"We'll supply you with a clean sheet," Aunt Henrietta said. "Everybody wears a sheet, man, woman, or child."

"Is there anything special I should dress in underneath?" Dale Blue asked and giggled.

"You wear underneath what you would to church," Aunt Cornelia said, disapproving.

The time for the baptism was four o'clock, and at three-thirty we filled up cars and started for the Greenbrier. Dale Blue, Dawson, and Uncle Henry had wrapped themselves in their sheets. The river was seven miles from the farm. We left the highway and wound on an unmarked blacktop road through a state forest and into a gorge which was already partly shaded by the west slope of the wooded mountain.

The green river was shallow and fast, no mud in it because the bottom was all stones that had been shaped by the current until they were rounded like Nana's loaves of Jesus bread. On the rocky beach cars were parked.

"If anybody had ever told me I'd be doing a crazy thing like this," Dale Blue said.

"Salvation's not crazy," Nana said.

"What if I get water up my nose?" Dale Blue asked.

"Just breathe out when you go under," Uncle Henry said.

"If I get water up my nose, I might need a trip to Greece too," she said.

She didn't like the crowd, not only kin, but also a good many of the congregation as well as some fishermen and a group of sight-seers. The thing that made her buck, though, was the photographer from Lewisburg who'd come because of Uncle Henry's reputation.

"No!" Dale Blue said, refusing to leave the Caddy. "He's not taking my picture! Suppose they see it in Sewickley. I couldn't show my face."

"Please, Dale Blue, for Momma," Uncle Henry pleaded.

"Not for anybody, not Dawson either, and not you if you remember who you are. They'll laugh you out of the Iron and Coal Club!"

She pulled the door shut, rolled up the window, and drew the sheet tight around herself. Uncle Henry circled the car begging her. Dawson was mad because he wanted to get into the river. The skinny photographer angled with his camera. He tried to take a picture of Dale Blue through the tinted windshield. She covered her face with her sheet. Uncle Henry, growing redder every second, ran him off, tripped on his sheet, and fell, showing for an instant his purple-and-white striped drawers, pale legs, and wine garters.

"That's enough," Nana, between Uncle Asa and Albert, said. "We'll leave."

"They can do it to me," Uncle Henry said. "I'm ready to go to the water."

"Me too," Dawson said.

"We'll go home," Nana said.

We moved among gawking people to get back into the cars, and like a funeral procession we drove to the farm, all except Uncle Henry who tore off in the Caddy with Dale Blue and Dawson. Nana again sat on the bench under the Indian cigar-tree. Family milled around, picked at the ham, and dribbled away home.

"What'll Henry do to Dale Blue?" my mother asked my daddy that night.

"What'd Henry ever do but turn it so she'd have an easy time kicking it?" my daddy asked.

"Turn what?" I asked.

"Sh-h-h," my mother said. "Go to bed."

Barking dogs woke me. Daddy carried his flashlight and shotgun outside to see about it. He thought a fox or coon was after our chickens, but the henhouse was quiet. Finally the dogs stopped barking, though they whined a while.

I thought Uncle Henry, Dale Blue, and Dawson were gone to Pittsburgh, but the next morning they drove to the farm. They kissed Nana and pretended nothing had happened. Uncle Henry joked with her. She sat under the tree without moving.

Dale Blue hummed and prissed about. She had on earrings shaped like sunflowers, and she wore a yellow shirt, yellow shorts, and yellow tennis shoes. Her legs were the prettiest I'd ever seen, all the hair smoothed off, the skin tan and satiny, like a dancing girl instead of a married woman. I got caught looking at her legs. She smiled at me, and there I was hot in the face again.

"We thought you'd left," my mother said.

"Oh we're going after while," Uncle Henry said. He was dressed like Dale Blue, yellow shorts, yellow shirt, though his tennis shoes were white. His lumpy muscled legs were funny with hair curled man-thick over them. "I want to show Dale Blue around. She hasn't had much chance to see the farm, especially the view."

"The view?" my daddy asked.

"From the silo," Uncle Henry said. "I told her you can see a lot of the valley from the silo."

My mother looked at my daddy who looked at her as I looked at them, and they looked at me. Not many people would climb our silo. I'd do it, yet the first time and the second time too I'd been scared because the silo, made of reinforced concrete slabs, was a hundred and twenty feet high.

You ducked into a vertical hatch and went up an iron ladder covered by a wooden canopy to protect climbers from wind and weather. It was like rising in a dim upright tunnel, and at the top was a sliding metal door not to see the view from but to blow in silage and for ventilation. Beams and boards had been laid across the slabs just under the galvanized dome. My mother would never climb the silo, and it'd been a long time since my daddy had.

"At least she's got nerve," my daddy said as Uncle Henry, Dawson, and Dale Blue crossed the pasture toward the barn. Uncle Henry slowed to swing a hand down and pick up a pebble. He fingered the pebble.

I ran after them. The hatch on the silo was inside the barn. Dawson, acting brave, claimed he wanted to be the first to go up, but Uncle Henry told him ladies first. Dale Blue was afraid she'd dirty her yellow shirt or shorts. She didn't like putting her hands on the rusty rungs. She made a face.

"I don't think I want to," she said.

"You'll love it," Uncle Henry said. "You can see so far your eyes get tired from the distance."

"Go on without me," she said.

"Hon, you know I like to share everything with you," he said.

Still making a face, she started up. Uncle Henry went after her, and me after Dawson. Since we were inside the wooden tunnel, we couldn't tell how high we'd climbed. Light came in only from cracks and from the opening at the top. We must've gone up a couple of minutes before Dale Blue got nervous.

"How far now?" she asked.

"We're close," Uncle Henry said, which was a lie.

"I'm tired," Dale Blue said after we climbed a while farther.

"Too much invested to stop now," Uncle Henry said. "Rest at the top."

"I don't think I like this," Dale Blue said. "We must be pretty high."

"You're pretty, high or low," Uncle Henry said. "And you'll forget the climb when you see the view."

Old Dawson wasn't talking much. Earlier he'd bragged about how he'd shinnied a rope up to the steel rafters of his school gym, but now all I heard was his breathing. I accidentally bumped against his leg and felt him trembling.

"Making it all right, city-freak?" I asked.

"Whew!" was the only thing he said.

At the top Dale Blue was really nervous. Her voice quivered.

"I'll help you up on the boards," Uncle Henry said.

"I don't like any of this," she said.

"Just ease on over," Uncle Henry said.

"Don't push!" she said.

He got her up on the boards, but he stayed on the ladder.

"Occurs to me they probably haven't replaced these boards and beams in years," Uncle Henry said. "Have they, Willie?"

"Not that I know about," I said.

"Hope they're not rotten," Uncle Henry said.

"Rotten!" Dale Blue said.

"Just look at that view, will you?" Uncle Henry said.

"The hell with the view!" Dale Blue said.

"You can see the old gristmill," Uncle Henry said.

"The hell with the old gristmill too," she said. "Am I on rotten boards?"

"Just don't move around a whole lot," Uncle Henry said. "It's higher than I remembered up here. Stick your head out the hole and look down, but be careful of the boards."

"No!" Dale Blue said.

"There's another way we can tell how high we are," Uncle Henry said. "I'll drop this pebble, and we'll see how long it takes to hit bottom."

He held out his hand and let go the pebble. I don't know, even for me who was used to the height, the pebble seemed to take about half an hour to hit. It caused a little plunk in the sour silage-mash, the plunk echoing in the hollowness of the dark silo.

"Get me down from here!" Dale Blue said.

"If you don't like the view, we can leave, but be careful of those boards," Uncle Henry said. "Don't move too much on those boards."

"Give me your hand!" Dale Blue said. "Henry?"

"You sound scared," he said.

"My teeth are clicking," she said.

"Momma, don't be afraid," Dawson said, but he was shivering on the ladder.

"Well I guess I'll help you down then," Uncle Henry said. "I forgot about those boards being up here so long they'd rot. Don't

move fast now. And there is one thing before I give you my hand.
You have to go to the river with me and Dawson."

"Damn you, Henry, don't you fool around with me up here!" she
said.

"Who's fooling?" he asked. "Just tell me you'll go, and I'll give
you my hand and help you down off those rotten boards which might
give under you any second if you move too much."

"Henry, you bastard, you get me down or I'll make you so sorry
you'll wish you lived under a rock!"

"I don't think you ought to talk to me like that, Dale Blue, not in
the situation you're in."

"The situation you're in is if you don't get me down off here in a
hurry I'll bust your ass!" she said.

"Let's climb down, boys," Uncle Henry said.

"You can't just leave her!" Dawson said.

"Henry, goddamn you, I'll go to the lawyers," Dale Blue said.
They'll take you tonsils to toenails."

"Your last opportunity," Uncle Henry said. "I'll help you off the
boards and down the ladder if you promise to go to the river with
Dawson and me. If you don't, you can come down by yourself. Now I
wouldn't start yelling too loud on those boards."

I was already backing when she screamed words at him I never
knew a woman could use. She didn't sound like herself, not only the
cussing, but her voice in the silo seemed to be coming from ten di-
rections at the same time. Dawson began crying. Uncle Henry had to
force him down.

"Go on, boy," Uncle Henry said. "Go on now."

After I reached bottom, she was still shouting. Dawson was carrying on too. My mother and father were running toward the barn.
Chickens squawked, cattle stampeded, and pigeons flapped so hard
they shed feathers.

"I'm going back up!" Dawson hollered and tried to get on the
ladder, but Uncle Henry dragged him away.

"Those beams and boards are all right," Uncle Henry said softly
to Dawson. "I climbed up last night. They'll hold."

Daddy and I looked at each other and nodded. The barking dogs were explained.

"But she might fall anyhow!" Dawson said, his face wet, his lips bubbling.

"You know I love her too much to hurt her," Uncle Henry said. "And she thinks too much of herself to fall."

Uncle Henry stayed at the barn but made the rest of us leave. My daddy had to pull Dawson. All morning and afternoon she hollered. At dark she still hadn't come down. Dawson was sent home with Aunt Henrietta and Uncle Albert. I lay in my bed hearing Dale Blue's voice carry over the pasture. She cussed, she screamed, she cried.

"Henry Sharp, you'll wish you were dead when I'm finished with you!" she hollered. "You'll wish you were in a meat grinder!"

Before sunup I was down the back steps on my bare feet and out the dining room window. I ran among cornstalks which rattled and bashed me. I snuck through mist to the barn where I hid behind bales of the new hay.

Dale Blue wasn't yelling any more. She wept and talked pitifully.

"What'd I ever do to make you treat me this way?" she asked.

"It's for your own good," Uncle Henry said. "Yours and everybody's own good."

"I bore your child and have tried to be a loving wife," she said.

"Come to the river with me, and I'll lay the world at your feet," Uncle Henry said up the silo.

"You go to hell on a Honda!" she wailed.

Daddy came to the barn, but Uncle Henry sent him back to the house. About mid-morning Uncle Henry called up to Dale Blue, who was sniffling.

"You want me to bring you your comb?" Uncle Henry called. "The photographer's going to be here after while."

"Who?" Dale Blue asked, and her voice echoed in the silo: who? who? who?

"That photographer from the Lewisburg paper," Uncle Henry said.

"No!" she sobbed.

"Can't stop the press," Uncle Henry said. "Now wouldn't it be better just to let me climb up there, bring you down so you can rest a while, and then we'll drive to the river?"

She whimpered.

"I love you," Uncle Henry called. "I'd rather die than be hurting you. Dale Blue, do this one thing for me."

"Henry, please come get me off these goddamn boards!" she cried.

He ran up that ladder after her and half carried her down. All the way she bawled. Her shorts weren't so yellow any longer, but most of her hair was still on top her head, though falling apart.

Uncle Henry kissed her a long time. He helped her across the pasture to the house, washed her off in the bathtub, and put her to bed in the spare room with the shades drawn.

Later my mother, Aunt Henrietta, and Aunt Cornelia got Dale Blue on her feet to dress her in her sheet. She, Dawson, and Uncle Henry were dipped by the Reverend Arbogast in the Greenbrier River at four-thirty. There was to be a party at the house, but Dale Blue wouldn't leave the Caddy. Uncle Henry had to drive her to White Sulphur. She was still hugging the sheet around her, and her wet hair had toppled.

The next morning sunshine and crows woke me. Something was different in the house. Downstairs the grandfather clock ticked and chimed. I sniffed the keen, charred odor of hickory and the warm, fermented scent of buttermilk biscuits rising from the old Kalamazoo. My stomach flipflopped. Whooping, I kicked the sheet straight up and grabbed for my jeans on the run to the kitchen.

A Darkness on the Mountain

Roy saw—really saw—Anna Mae during a church meeting which started on a summer afternoon. The meetinghouse was in a narrow, wooded valley where tulip poplar trees cast down a deep shade. Nearby was a fast, clear river formed by cold mountain streams. Roy, his parents, and his young sister had driven over in his mud-splattered Chevy.

He had parked in the shade among other dirty, dilapidated cars. While his sister and parents went inside, he joined men squatting under a tree. They smoked, spat, and listened to hymn-singing coming from open windows.

The meetinghouse, constructed by the congregation, was an unpainted frame building with a tarpaper roof. The four corners were held off the ground by cinder blocks. Haslip, the preacher, had been able to talk the electric company into bringing in a power line from the highway. There was a steeple but no bell.

The meeting didn't get going good until dusk. Some of the men around Roy went inside and others came out, wiping sweat off their faces. In low voices they talked of coal. When hymns were not being sung, Roy heard the darkening river bubble over rocks. Occasionally a rattling car or pickup approached with a family.

Roy had looked at Anna Mae before, but that was not the same as seeing her. She followed her father and mother. Her father used crutches, and, as she waited behind him at the door, she was lighted by a bug-pinged overhead bulb. No longer was she stringy but had filled out into curves and moved with a careful, gliding step. She had on black slippers and a white cotton dress which was tight around her waist. Her black hair was tied at the back of her neck with a white ribbon. She smiled in what to Roy was a mysterious yet knowledgeable female way.

He stared at her until she was inside. He finished his cigarette, rose, and entered. The few seats in the meetinghouse had been unbolted from an old school bus and were being sat on by elderly women who fanned themselves, sang, and clapped to the music. The musicians—three men in shirtsleeves playing a guitar, a banjo, and an accordion—sweated at the front of the room. Roy's father, stern and gaunt, was song leader. He called out the words in his strong, deep voice and beat the heel of a hand against a jingling tambourine.

Roy stood near the door. The room was hot and close. Colored pictures of Jesus had been nailed to wall studs. Voices around him lifted shrilly. Anna Mae sat between her parents. Her red lips moved. She turned and looked at him. She was still singing, but her mouth was smiling. The smile seemed a taunt.

The building pulsated with the thumping music. The accordion sparkled, and the tambourines flashed. Haslip, the preacher, was climbing onto a platform hammered together from scrap lumber. His eyelids, like Roy's and most of the men's, were darkened by fine coal that miners call "bug dust." It was like eye shadow. Haslip's white shirt was unbuttoned at the collar. He glistened with sweat.

"This is a place for believers in Hell's fire!" he called. "If you don't believe in Hell's fire, get out of here!"

Roy didn't listen to the words. He kept his eyes on Anna Mae. Her face was raised to the platform, her mouth open a little. When Haslip threatened doom and damnation, her expression became prettily alarmed. She kept her lips moistened. Roy knew she knew he was looking at her.

After the preaching and hymns ended, he was first out of the meeting. He waited along the path. Anna Mae walked beside her father. She passed just a few inches in front of Roy. He smelled her perfume. It was like honeysuckle. She got into the cab of the pickup truck. He could no longer see her for the dark.

"What you doing just standing here?" his sister asked him.

"I don't have to be doing nothing to be standing," he answered her, shamed at being caught. He hurried to his Chevy.

He didn't go calling until the next Saturday. When he drove home from the mine, he had him a bath in a galvanized tub on the back porch of the weathered Jenny Lind house. He scrubbed coal dust off himself with brown soap and a stiff brush. He put on his meeting suit, a black wool he'd bought from J.C. Penney's in Bluefield. He attempted to leave without being noticed, but his mother and sister came after him.

"Where you going dressed up for preaching?" his mother asked. A wrinkled woman, she had graying straight hair and sunken blue eyes. Through the winter she'd been sick and hadn't regained her weight. Her green dress fitted loosely.

"Just going," he answered and hurried down the wooden steps to his Chevy to prevent them from questioning him further.

He drove to Anna Mae's. Like him, she lived in a one-story structure, more cabin than house, set on the side of a wooded mountain. Stones carried from a stream leveled the two front corners. To the side was a garden plot with corn and snap beans growing in it. A goat was tied to a locust tree, and chickens pecked around the porch.

Roy climbed steps made from slate slabs fitted into dirt. On the porch was Anna Mae's father. He rocked in a cane-bottomed chair. His crutches leaned against the house. He was a large man who, since he'd stopped loading coal, had gone to fat, Soft, pale flesh hung off him. A pantleg was folded up and fastened by a safety pin.

He'd lost his leg by backing into the whirling blade of a Joy cutter. The Joy had sliced so neatly and quickly he hadn't realized the leg was gone, even though he was falling. He received compensation from the company and a pension from the union. As a result, he could live without having to work.

"Roy," he said. He spat over the rail of the porch into the yard.

He shifted the wad of tobacco in his cheek.

"We could use a rain," Roy answered, not taking a chair but squatting against one of the round wooden posts which held up the porch roof. By turning his head, he could see the road over which he'd just driven and beyond to the next mountain, which rose like a steep green wave. Crows flew above the ridge, their cawing faint.

" 'Tis a fact," Anna Mae's father agreed. "Things is dry."

Roy was facing the father, pretending to be interested in what was said, but really listening to tell whether Anna Mae was inside. He heard nothing there. He tried to sense it. The father's words came slow and easy. He spat off the porch. Roy waited.

Soundlessly Anna Mae appeared at the screen door. She was wearing the white cotton dress. He smelled the honeysuckle perfume. He guessed she'd put on both the dress and the perfume for him.

"Hello, Roy," she said and smiled.

"Hello, Anna Mae."

She continued to stand at the door. He didn't look at her again, nor she at him. After a time she stepped back quietly into the house. Roy remained another thirty minutes before saying good-by to the father and going home.

He next saw Anna Mae with her parents at the meeting Sunday morning. He went early so he could nod to her out front. After dinner he slipped away from his mother and sister to drive to Anna Mae's house.

She, her father, and her mother were on the porch. The mother was a pleasant, heavy woman whose feet spread in her shoes. She dipped snuff, and her lip was drawn as if she had no upper teeth. Roy squatted against the post. Anna Mae sat on the swing, toeing herself and humming.

He talked politely to the parents. The dry heat settled around them. They watched each car on the road. Flies buzzed. Anna Mae entered the house. She came out with a bushel basket.

"I'll pick them roasting ears," she said to her mother, but it was meant for Roy, and he knew it.

"Reckon I'll help Anna Mae," he told the parents.

He stood, and as he walked off the porch after her, he was aware of the eyes on him. The eyes made him feel unnatural. He stumbled over his own feet. Anna Mae laughed.

He held the basket while she twisted ears of corn off the stalks. He followed her up and down rows, secretly glancing at the whiteness of her neck and the curve of her dress over her hips. Pollen fell and made him sneeze. When the basket was full, he carried it to the kitchen door for her.

Her hands touched his on the basket's wire handles. She smiled at him before going inside. He remembered the touch as he drove home and as he lay on his bed in the night.

The mine didn't work the next week. Roy and his father sawed down trees, skinned them, and snaked them out to the road by using a drag chain and a mule named Billy. There wasn't much money in timbering, but it was better than just sitting around waiting to load coal.

His father mentioned Anna Mae. He and Roy were eating a lunch of soda crackers, sardines, and orange pop. They had kept the pop cold by leaning it against rocks in a stream.

"You courting?" the father asked. He was sitting on a log, peering at Roy. The greenish-gray eyes in the gaunt face made Roy feel his insides were being fingered.

"I reckon," he answered.

His father continued to eat, his jaw moving thoroughly and mechanically. When he finished, he stood and walked to the mule.

"I got no objections," he said, "but I don't want no funny business."

Roy's mother also knew about Anna Mae. The mother fussed at him for his dirty fingernails and his need of a haircut. She made him drive her to Bluefield where she took him into J.C. Penney's to buy a brown summer suit. He also bought a pearl-colored hat. He wore both the new suit and hat when he went calling on Anna Mae the next Saturday.

Before he reached the house he saw the red car. It was a shiny new

Ford which had mudguards with ruby reflectors, chrome side mirrors, and whip antennas poking out of the rear fenders. With V-8 engine roaring and horn blaring, the Ford had sped around Roy's old Chevy a bunch of times.

Roy climbed the slate steps to the house. Buster Beard was on the porch with Anna Mae and her parents. The youngest of five Beard brothers, Buster was blond and pretty. Instead of wearing a suit like Roy, he had on a yellow shirt, black-and-red checked slacks, and a pair of sharp-toed brown-and-white shoes. His sideburns were long. He grinned at Roy.

Roy knew him. They were the same age and worked at the mine. Buster, though, like his brothers, was a heller. He spent all his money on cars, clothes, and women. He'd get the girls in the car with him, and they'd plead for him to slow down as he fishtailed around mountain curves. They would cover their eyes and scream. After he scared them half to death, he parked on fire trails. The girls were then too weak to resist him. More than one father would have come after Buster with a shotgun had it not been for the brothers.

Neither Buster nor his brothers ever went to church meetings. Instead, they hung around roadhouses on the Kentucky border where Saturdays the whole family got drunk. The oldest brother, a giant with a scar on his face, had been in the state prison for shooting a man. When the Beards walked into a place, brawls had a way of being born.

Roy squatted on the porch in the spot against the post he had come to feel was his. Anna Mae stared at the floor. Her parents' faces were solemn. Buster was talking as if nothing were unusual. He always ran off at the mouth. He liked to show his white teeth which he went to a tooth doctor for to get cleaned. Though his blond hair was not messed, he kept smoothing his hand over the top of it.

"That's a hotdoggity hat you got on there, Roy," Buster said, mocking. "A pearl hat like that's bound to make us some rain. Why, water'd run uphill to get on a hat like that."

Roy's face burned. He couldn't find words. Buster laughed at him and blabbed on. He talked about the persimmon trees being heavy with fruit. He said the hornets were building their nests high this summer, so look out for a mean winter. He'd found some bear tracks at the lick. When Buster was not speaking, the silence seemed as long as a day.

Anna Mae announced she was going to the spring for water. Roy stood quickly to walk with her. Buster, too, came along. They walked on either side of her. Buster was whistling and cutting his eyes at Anna Mae.

The spring was behind the house. Water dripped from a mossy cavern into a wooden bucket. The bucket was almost full. Roy reached it before Buster. Buster laughed.

"Why sure," he said. "You carry the bucket, and I'll carry Anna Mae."

With that, he swept his arms under her and swung her from the ground. She whooped. While Roy gawked, Buster began to spin. Anna Mae's white dress slid over her knees. She pushed it down. She had an arm around Buster's neck.

She started laughing and begged Buster to let her down. He kept spinning. She hit at his chest, but each time she turned loose of her dress it slipped off her knees. Buster spun until Anna Mae collapsed in his arms. She put her head down on his shoulder and her mouth against his shirt. When Buster finally released her, she was staggering. She had to lean on Buster to steady herself.

Roy was still holding the bucket. He was so angry he could hear his blood. He would never have dared touch Anna Mae like that. As they returned to the house, he marched silently. Anna Mae was flushed and breathless. Without saying good-by to her, Roy left the bucket at the kitchen door and went down the mountain to his Chevy. It looked like a piece of junk next to Buster's shiny new Ford.

Roy drove along the road a mile and pulled off onto the cinder shoulder. Below him the mountain sloped to a laurel thicket and from the thicket to a creek. He sat in the Chevy until after five o'clock. At that time he heard the sound of Buster's V-8. Roy got out and stood in the road. Buster saw him and braked. Tires skidded across cinders. Even before the Ford completely stopped, Buster was opening the door.

"You looking for me?" he asked.

"She's my girl," Roy said.

"She don't act like it none."

"Whether she acts like it or not, you keep away."

"I'm not doing nothing unless she tells me."

Roy swung as if throwing a rock. The blow didn't hit solid because Buster was expecting it and raised his arm. They fought along the edge of the road. Although Buster was taller, Roy was as strong. They slugged toe to toe until their faces were bloody.

As they became arm weary, they wrestled. Heaving and lunging, they toppled over the bank. Briers snagged Roy's new suit, and Buster's yellow shirt was smudged. They fought through the laurel thicket, biting and kicking. They crashed out of the thicket and rolled to the creek. They sprawled on the ground, panted, and glared at one another.

Buster rose first and climbed toward the road. Roy followed. Both had to stop for breath. Buster, wiping his face with a handkerchief, drove away. Roy dusted off his torn new suit. His pearl hat lay crushed in the cinders.

He waited until dark before driving home. He wanted to be sure his father was in bed. As Roy washed himself quietly, his mother came into the kitchen. She put a thin hand to her mouth but said nothing for fear of rousing the father. They heard him snoring. She dabbed at Roy's face with the wet end of a towel.

She made him strip off his suit so she could sponge out the dirt and stains. She brought her sewing basket and threaded a needle. When Roy went to bed, she was still bent over the kitchen table, working on the suit.

In the morning he was stiff. He looked at his face in a mirror which hung from a nail in his small bedroom. Cuts and bruises were on his cheeks, chin, and forehead, and the skin around his eyes was black. He couldn't avoid his father. He walked into the kitchen and sat at the table where his father and sister were at breakfast. They stared at Roy. His mother, frightened, turned from the stove.

"Who done it?" the father demanded.

Roy told. He had once received a beating from his father with a thick leather miner's belt. The skin of his buttocks had been split and blood had run down his legs. He'd never lied since.

He believed he might have another beating coming, but his father sat silently, both fists on the table, and when he spoke, he didn't deepen his voice.

"I don't want no more trouble," the father said. "You stay away from the Beards. Them's my words."

They went to the meeting that morning. Roy's mother had fixed his new suit so he could wear it. People blinked at the sight of his face. Anna Mae kept glancing at him during the preaching, her eyes wide.

That afternoon he sat on the porch of his house. He wore his pants and undershirt. His parents and sister had gone visiting. He heard the red Ford coming down the road. It zoomed by, the horn blowing. It was headed in Anna Mae's direction.

Roy dressed and drove to Bluefield. At a shopping center he bought a box of chocolate-covered cherries. He drove back to Anna Mae's house. The red Ford was parked in front.

Carrying the candy, he climbed the steps. Anna Mae, her parents, and Buster were on the porch. Roy looked at Buster's face. It was as badly marked and misshapen as his own, but Buster was grinning.

Roy handed the box of chocolate-covered cherries to Anna Mae. She thanked him, tore off the cellophane, and passed the box to her parents, to him, and to Buster. She set the box on a chair beside Buster.

Buster began to eat. He didn't take one or two pieces of candy. He took a dozen. The sweet juice ran out of his mouth and over his chin. By the time he was finished, the box was nearly empty. Roy was outraged. Buster grinned.

Neither of them got to walk with Anna Mae to the spring because a summer storm blew in. They saw dark clouds sweeping over the mountains and lightning flashing into the forest. Big drops of rain slapped leaves and forced everybody into the house. The air was suddenly cold.

They sat in the front room which had linoleum on the floor, a hole in the wall for a stovepipe, and tasseled pillows on the pink leatherette sofa. Buster and Anna Mae were next to each other on the sofa. Buster was telling stories, laughing, and snapping his fingers. Anna Mae laughed with him. In spite of themselves, her parents smiled. Buster was winning them over.

Roy sat quiet on the edge of a straight chair, his arms folded, until he could suffer no more. Rising, he said he had to leave. Anna Mae again thanked him for the candy, but she didn't try to talk him out of going. He drove down the road a mile and parked on the cindered shoulder.

He had a long wait. Either Anna Mae or her parents must've invited Buster to supper, for it was well after dark before Roy heard the car coming. Rain was still falling. He turned on his headlights and stood in front of them.

As Buster drew up, Roy was reaching into his pocket for his knife. Buster came out of his car with his, catching the blade in his teeth and jerking it open. They circled between the cars. The headlights threw their shadows onto the wet road and slope of the mountain.

"You mean you're going to try to put holes in me with that frog sticker?" Buster asked.

"I'm going to cut out your gizzard," Roy answered.

He lunged. Buster danced away. They continued circling, their arms extended in crablike fashion, their backs hunched. At the same moment they rushed. Their bodies joined hip to shoulder. As they broke, Roy felt the blade come into him. He hollered, and his knife dropped. Blood spurted from a hole in his coat at the upper part of his left arm. He grabbed the wound.

Buster stepped back, laughed, and cleaned his knife by sticking it into the ground. He snapped the blade shut. Returning to his car, he crowed like a rooster. He roared off down the road, tires hissing and red lights flashing.

With a bloody hand Roy opened the Chevy trunk. He found a rope and twisted it around his arm to slow the bleeding. Slowly he drove home.

Before entering his house, he removed his coat and shirt. Blood oozed. He slapped cold water from the spring against the wound and again tightened the rope. He crept through the kitchen to his room without switching on any lights. He hid his wet, bloody suit under the bed. He half fell to the covers but protected his throbbing arm.

In the morning he stayed in bed. He was weak, his stomach queasy. At least the bleeding had stopped. He stuffed the rope under his pillow and pulled a blanket over himself. When his father came in, Roy kept his arm out of sight.

"I don't feel so good," he said. "I think I better lie up today."

The father's greenish-gray eyes gazed at him, and the father put a calloused hand on Roy's forehead.

"All right," the father said. "The mine ain't working anyway. I'll get somebody else to help me timber."

Roy didn't allow his mother to see the arm until the father had left the house. She cried as her tender, trembling fingers felt around the wound. She hurried to the kitchen and came back with a pan of steaming water. Using a towel, she soaked the arm, keeping the water as hot as he could stand it. His sister watched fearfully. When the wound was clean and pink, the mother wrapped on a bandage torn from an old shirt.

She carried him vegetable soup for lunch. He swallowed a few sips. He had slept most of the morning, and he dropped off again in the afternoon. At dark he opened his eyes. His father was sitting quietly beside the bed. The father stood, unwrapped the bandage, and inspected the wound.

"I ought to flay the hide right off you," the father said. "I told you to keep away from them Beards. Now you listen to the Word. I'm going to read it, and you listen."

And he got the Bible.

Roy didn't leave the house that week. He slept late, ate the food his mother cooked, and sat on the porch. Each day his mother washed the wound and changed the bandage. The cut in his arm was healing without infection. Already the lips of the cut had started to close. He flexed his fingers and exercised his arm so it wouldn't stiffen on him. By the end of the week he could use it enough to help his mother and sister with chores.

Sitting on the porch Saturday afternoon, he heard the red Ford coming down the road. He stopped rocking. The car sped by in a snarling rush of wind. Twenty minutes later it returned. He glimpsed Anna Mae in the front seat beside Buster. She wore her white cotton dress and a white ribbon in her dark hair. Roy looked in the direction the Ford had gone long after the sound of it faded.

"What you going to do?" his sister whispered to him.

"Nothing," he said. "I ain't going to do nothing."

The Ford didn't come back until late that night. He lay awake listening for it. Buster had probably taken her to a movie in Bluefield. Roy clenched his fists and eyes in the dark. He wouldn't let himself believe Anna Mae had allowed herself to be taken on the fire trail.

In spite of his arm, he was ready to load coal on Monday. He put on his coveralls, steel-toed shoes, and a helmet to which a lamp could be attached. He drove his father to the non-union doghole on the side of the mountain. Big International, Mack, and White trucks had worn ruts deep into the ground. Muddy water stood in some of the ruts.

Buster and his four brothers were smoking a last cigarette at the entry. The brothers were larger and meatier looking than Buster. As Roy and his father passed, one of the Beards snickered. Roy felt his father's hand urge him on into the mine.

"Don't hear them scum," the father said to Roy as they stooped to walk the haulway. "Their bones will fuel Hell's boilers."

That night after his parents were asleep, Roy unfastened the screen of his bedroom window and slipped to the ground, his bare feet in the cool grass taking his weight softly. He allowed the Chevy to coast downhill before starting the engine. He drove two miles and parked up a hollow.

Carrying a short-handled, low-coal shovel, he left the Chevy and moved up through the woods and down into the next hollow where Buster and his brothers lived in an old ramshackle house that had belonged to their mother. The mother had died during the winter, and the funeral was the only place anybody had ever seen Beards act respectable. They stayed respectable maybe even a whole hour after she was in the ground.

The house was dark. The moon glinted on car hulks abandoned

around it. Roy waited at the edge of the woods until he heard the Ford. It bounced and its springs squeaked along the potted road. Headlights flashed through the trees. When Buster cut the engine, switched off the headlights, and stepped out, Roy darted behind him and rapped him on the skull with the flat of the shovel.

Buster slumped. Roy caught him and stood watching the house. No lights came on. He picked up the shovel, shouldered Buster, and hurried into the woods. He lowered Buster and twisted stove wire around his wrists before lifting him and climbing.

At the Chevy he dumped Buster on the floorboards in the rear and drove seventy-three miles to the Kentucky border. He turned into a hollow almost blocked with weeds and sumac. Buster had been moaning and calling. Roy opened the door and pulled him out by his feet so Buster's body bumped against the ground.

"What you doing to me, Roy?" Buster asked.

Roy didn't answer. He filled the reservoir of his old carbide lamp in a stream and attached the lamp to his helmet. Roughly he stood Buster and shoved him. They followed a tram road which led up the mountain. Ties had decayed. Against the sky was the jagged outline of a tumbledown headhouse. They were winded when they reached it.

"You going to kill me?" Buster asked, his wrists still tied behind him.

Again Roy didn't speak but shoved Buster ahead of him toward the entry to the deserted mine. As they moved into blackness, Roy dropped a chip of carbide into his lamp, adjusted the feed, and spun the flint wheel. The lamp hissed into brilliant white light.

The haulway was wet. They walked bent over to keep from hitting the roof. At times the haulway was almost clogged by piles of rock and slate. Old timbers were splintered. Water dripped, and they had to jump dark puddles. Buster's fancy sharp-toed shoes were ruined. He slowed and tried to speak. Roy pushed him on.

They went deep into the mine. Roy found a room where the coal pillars hadn't been completely pulled. He forced Buster down and tied his ankles with wire. He then arched Buster's back so that when the ankles and wrists were joined by wire, there was tension on it. Lastly, Roy strung wire around a rotting prop. If Buster pulled too hard against the prop, chances were the mountain would settle on him.

"You really ain't going to leave me here, are you?" Buster asked.

Without answering, Roy examined the wire and left the room.

"Hey, Roy, listen, for God's sake!" Buster shouted.

Roy walked on. Buster kept calling. He was in a darkness that never lifted. He was almost screaming. For a long time Roy heard him. Finally there was no sound except the dripping of water.

Roy went to the Chevy and drove back across the border. When he got to his house, he passed it, turned around, and coasted in on a dead engine, the headlights off. Quietly he washed himself in the spring before climbing through the window to his bed.

The next morning at work, the four Beard brothers came through the mine looking for Buster. They roamed the haulways, questioning men and checking rooms. Later they organized a search of the woods around their house.

During the night Roy lay on the floor near the wall instead of using his bed. He listened to night sounds and watched for dark shapes at his window. He slept little.

The following afternoon as he and his father were cutting coal, the four Beard brothers came out of the mine darkness. Each had a lamp on his helmet and was hunchbacked because of the roof's height. Roy's father became motionless.

The brothers walked toward Roy. He reached for his ax. Then the sheriff was pushing among them. He was a big-bellied ex-miner with a bulldog face. He carried a .38 revolver in his hip pocket, and his hand was on that pocket.

"All right, you got your business and I got mine," the sheriff said to the Beard brothers.

"You better attend to it," the oldest Beard, the one named Odell who had a scar on his face, answered. "If you don't, we do."

"Just scratch on out of here and let me do it," the sheriff told them. "What you think the taxpayers support me for?"

The brothers backed off and seeped into the blackness. Roy was still holding the ax. His father hadn't moved. The sheriff wiped his arm across his mouth.

"Roy, if you know anything, anything at all, you better tell me," he said. "Otherwise I can't make no guarantees."

"I don't know nothing," Roy answered.

"I hope not," the sheriff said. "For your sake I sure God hope not."

After the sheriff left, Roy had to face his father. Each squinted in the light from the other's lamp. At least Roy didn't have to see his father's eyes.

"You mixed up in it?" the father asked. "Don't lie to me now."

"Not me, Pa, honest, I'm not."

He didn't want to lie, but he'd gone too far to have a choice.

The sheriff took charge of the search for Buster. He led men into the mountains. A deputy discovered what he believed was a newly dug grave. Instead of a body they found a metal keg of white lightning. The deputies shot holes in it.

On the third morning as Roy moved along the haulway of the mine, a trolley hummed to life in a crackling shower of sparks and rumbled toward him. He squeezed against the coal. Iron sides of the loaded cars passed so close they nudged buttons on Roy's coveralls. Buster's brother Odell was at the controls.

"You ought to be more careful there, Roy," Odell said. "Something bad might happen to you."

Roy waited until after midnight before slipping from the window of his room. He ran barefooted to his Chevy and eased off the brake to let the car coast away from the house. He started the engine and drove toward the Kentucky border. He stopped twice to see if he was being followed. There were no other cars.

At the abandoned mine he climbed the old tram road, lighted his carbide lamp, and hurried into the deeper blackness. Even before reaching the room, he heard Buster. Buster's voice was weak and hoarse from screaming. Buster was filthy and stinking. He lay whimpering.

"Oh, Jesus, you come back," Buster said. "I thought you was never coming back. Rats been smelling and running over me. They was up to my face. Don't leave me, Roy. Please, Roy, don't leave me again!"

"You got to swear an oath," Roy said.

"I'll swear! I'll swear anything you say!"

Roy untwisted the wires from around the rotted prop and Buster's ankles. Buster couldn't stand by himself. Roy helped him up. Buster staggered and moaned. He cried. Roy guided him out.

"Oh them rats!" Buster whimpered.

He fell twice going down the tram road. His clothes were torn, his skin blackened. His wrists were still wired behind him, but at the stream he dropped to his knees and threw himself on his stomach to wiggle forward like a snake. He sucked water noisily.

Roy put him in the Chevy and drove him across the border. As they neared the cemetery on the mountainside, Roy switched off the headlights. The tombstones were slanted and ghostly. He shoved Buster to his mother's grave.

"Get on your knees and swear!" Roy ordered him. "Swear you'll never see Anna Mae no more. Swear before God and on this grave that if you break your word, your mother will fry in Hell's fire. The devils will drag her down there and burn her forever. She'll curse your name!"

Weeping in the moonlight, Buster swore. Roy kept him on his knees.

"You don't never tell where you been," Roy said. "You make up a story. If you even mention my name, your mother burns. Now swear it!"

When Roy finally let him up, Buster was bawling and staggering. Roy twisted the wire from his wrists and walked to the Chevy. Buster would have to get home on his own.

Roy drove to his house and climbed into his room. Again he lay on the floor listening instead of sleeping in his bed. The next morning he didn't go to work. He told his father the arm was hurting, and after the father left, Roy hid among laurel so he could watch the road. No Beard brothers came. The oath was holding.

On Friday when he went to work with his father in the mine, Roy never for a second turned his back to the room entry. He watched for the Beards to spring on him out of the darkness.

He needn't have been so careful. Men were already whispering about how in a roadhouse Buster had met three Kentuckians who talked him into going to a cockfight, got him liquored up, robbed him, and left him in an abandoned mine. Buster hadn't known where he was and wandered through the woods. He'd finally come onto a highway and hitchhiked home.

Near quitting time, Roy passed him setting brattices. Buster shied against the coal until Roy was by.

Saturday Roy bought a new pearl hat in Bluefield and put on the new suit his mother had again mended. He drove to Anna Mae's. She was surprised to see him. She came out onto the porch. He squatted by his post, and she sat on the swing, though she didn't toe it. Her hands rested on her lap.

There was a haze on the green mountains, and turkey buzzards spiraled in the air currents above the ridges. Each time Anna Mae heard a car approaching, she raised her eyes hopefully. None of the cars, however, was a red Ford with ruby-encrusted mudguards and whip antennas. After a while she'd get used to the idea that it wasn't coming any longer. Until then, Roy could wait.

A Southern Sojourn

It was mostly boredom and loneliness, for Orson was a conscientious man. His company sent him from Minnesota to Virginia to supervise the installation of a boiler in a new knitting mill. He found that mill located in the country—among dusty pines and dry broomstraw. The county seat, with the inevitable neo-classical courthouse under mossy oaks, had only six hundred inhabitants.

There was one motel, a ten-unit structure built of yellow stucco and named the Dixie. He rented a room by the week. Stones along the drive were painted white, and on the dry grass a shiny metal ball was supported by a concrete pedestal, the ball catching sunlight and flashing it against the stucco. He did have a TV in his room but was able to receive only one station, Lynchburg, and that fuzzily.

"We don't have a stoplight in the county," Haden, the man who owned the motel, said. "Nor a movie."

At first the place seemed quaint and idyllic. Orson wrote long letters to his wife, taking pains with his descriptions of the hot land and country people. He had plenty of time to compose letters. Shipments of boiler parts were late. He could sit at his desk and look busy while he wrote.

Each evening after work he returned to the motel, showered, and drank a gin. He went to the restaurant where Haden served a specialty of fried ham and oysters. Haden was having difficulty finding help for his kitchen.

"I can't pay them much," he said. By "them" he meant blacks. "But I have to compete with welfare. You want to buy a restaurant?"

After dinner Orson sat in a metal chair on the grass until mosquitoes drove him into his room. He read his mail and newspapers. He watched the fuzzy TV. On Sundays he attended the Presbyterian church. By the third week all that he'd considered quaint and idyllic was gone. At the end of the month he worried he was drinking too much.

He tried driving to Lynchburg, fifty miles away. He went to movies and ate at a hotel which served supposedly fine food, but it was nothing like Minneapolis or Chicago. He wanted his wife to come down. She, however, had the children and the new house.

He certainly wasn't looking for women. Friday evening as he sat on the grass in front of the motel he was aware only that he was hot and sticky in spite of his shower. He dreaded going to his room and lying on the unfriendly bed.

Eunice—Haden pronounced it with the accent on the second syllable—came from the kitchen carrying a galvanized can of trash. She was the new cook and waitress, a Negress maybe twenty-five or so. She wore a green uniform Haden provided and white tennis shoes.

She emptied the can into a wire incinerator and lit the trash with a match. A waxy milk carton flared, twisted, and fell to the ground. Fire spread into the dry broomstraw. She stamped it with her tennis shoes. Orson went to help.

"You'll ruin your shoes," he said.

"Don't I know."

"Stay back and let me do it."

She was thin but strong looking, her face long and narrow, her kinky hair dark and shiny. Heat had brought sweat to her face. Her skin was very black.

He put out the fire and wiped his hands on his handerchief. She stood holding the can.

"Next time use a top on the incinerator," he said.

"What top?"

"Well for the moment you're okay."

He started away, expecting her to thank him, but she said nothing. When he turned to look, she'd gone back inside the kitchen.

He didn't dwell upon her. He saw her almost every morning and evening when she came to the table to wait on him, but he never thought of anything else until the night after work he sat alone in the restaurant. She stood at the counter adding his bill. The counter pushed into her stomach. Her leg sagged, the knee bent inward so that her body was pulled to a curve. He was startled by her attractiveness.

He left the restaurant quickly. Even if he felt sorry for her, to take her out was unthinkable. Not that it had anything to do with her being black. He'd gone to school with Negroes, and there was little feeling in his father's house about color. Through the church, Orson had worked with underprivileged children in Minneapolis. But he was married and had two fine sons.

Get on the plane, he thought.

He flew home that weekend after trying to telephone his wife. She never answered, but he decided to chance it and surprise her. When he reached his new brick house, nobody answered the door to his ringing.

He let himself in and telephoned around the neighborhood to find she'd driven the children to visit her mother in Duluth. A rain settled over the house. He sat alone on the bed.

He wasn't able to reach her until late, and he agreed she shouldn't drive home at that hour in the rain. She came in early Sunday, but because of the children she could manage little time for him. He had his plane to catch. He left feeling irritable and harried.

Back in Virginia he would not think of Eunice. He closed his mind to her. Often Haden waited on tables, and she stayed in the kitchen. Orson glimpsed her standing at a stove, a white cloth around her hair.

On Wednesday the mill held a Fourth of July picnic. He stopped by the recreation area. It was located on the banks of a muddy, slow-flowing river. Men broke chunks of ice over beer in tubs.

Drinking, Orson watched the games, listened to the speech by the local congressman, and played horseshoes. Pretty girls waded in the river. Everyone was, of course, nice to him, but he didn't feel one of the crowd. There was always a barrier. The Civil War maybe. His Yankeeness and better pay. He wasn't sure, but the barrier existed.

He drank too much beer. He wasn't drunk, yet he was laughing loudly and realized it. He slipped away, returned to the motel, and tried to call his wife. There was no answer. She'd probably taken the children to the pool.

He hadn't eaten anything. He didn't want to go to the motel restaurant but was afraid of driving elsewhere. He crossed the grass, saw his distorted image in the metal ball on the concrete pedestal, and entered the restaurant. He was relieved to see Haden behind the cash register.

Haden, a fat, fair-skinned man with thin dark hair, sat with him while he ate. Haden wore a red sport shirt. He talked of fishing and the need for rain. In the south rain always seemed to be needed. Water just sank through the soil without leaving it wet.

"The earth's cracking open," Haden said. "We're all going to fall in."

At that moment a siren shrilled, an alarm calling the volunteer fire department. Haden stood and hurried to the door. Orson moved to go with him, but Haden motioned him back.

"Finish your meal. We got plenty of people just looking for something to do. Probably nothing but a field fire anyhow."

Haden drove away in his pickup truck, the tires throwing gravel. Orson sat and ate the last of his ham. He dropped a dime in the bejeweled jukebox. He found himself looking at the kitchen door.

Eunice came out and walked to his table. Her green uniform was clean and pressed. She smelled of perfume.

"Dessert?"

"Another glass of tea."

She walked to the kitchen. He fingered his pencil, pulled a paper napkin from the metal dispenser, and wrote in precise block letters, WILL YOU SHARE MY LONELINESS?

She came carrying his tea from the kitchen. When she set it on the table, he raised his hand with the napkin. She didn't understand. Questioning, she took the napkin, saw the printing, and read.

He sat still. He felt flushed and heady. She didn't look at him. Instead she studied the note as if having difficulty interpreting it. Music played from the jukebox. Though her head was still, her looped costume earrings still swung.

"You don't want me to," she said.

"I want you to."

"I don't think so."

"I'll drive down the road. When you get off work, I'll be parked."

Before she answered, a customer entered, a tourist who asked for a room. She folded the napkin into her uniform pocket and got a registration card. Orson stood, left a tip, and walked to the cash register. She added his bill.

"I'll be down the road," he said and counted money into her palm, which was tinted pink.

He walked out feeling lightheaded. He crossed to his room, washed his face, and brushed his teeth. As he combed his hair in front of the mirror, he was surprised to see he was smiling—a silly lopsided smile.

At nine-thirty he went to his car. Before starting it, he thought, It's not too late to go back. If I don't appear, she'll just walk the road as always. He reached to the ignition, hesitated, and turned the key. The Chrysler engine bubbled richly in the night.

He drove around the restaurant and looked toward the kitchen. A shadow passed the screen door, but he couldn't tell whether or not it was Eunice. He guided the car from the gravel drive to the highway and along it until he came to a rest area under pines—a picnic table and a dark refuse pail nailed to a post. There was a smell of fire.

He lit a cigarette, switched on the radio, and glanced back through the window. Of course she could have a boyfriend—some big buck with a knife or razor. Orson might end up bleeding and in a ditch. Stop thinking in stereotypes, he told himself.

He turned the music down. For an instant he again considered his wife and family. He shook his head. This had nothing to do with them. He'd lived in too many lonely rooms.

At a few minutes after ten he saw Eunice coming. She walked the weedy shoulder of the road. Her posture was erect. A car lighted her from behind and threw her elongated shadow across the ground. She appeared as flat as her shadow. He opened the door.

"You really think I'm going to get in there with you?" she asked.

"I think you might as well ride as walk."

"You know what people around here would do if they found you waiting for me?"

"They don't have to know."

"Suppose I want them to? Suppose I don't want to sneak around in the bushes?"

"Get in and we can talk about it."

She started away, came back, and slid in, her uniform rustling against the seat. When he reached across her to close the door, he smelled soap and perfume. She eyed him, her hands on her lap.

As the radio played, he drove onto the highway.

"Is there anyplace you'd like to go?" he asked.

"I'd like to go to the Commonwealth Club for cocktails and to the Country Club of Virginia for Lobster Thermidor."

He laughed.

"You like the way I talk?" she asked.

"I like it."

"Different from what you expected?"

"I guess so."

"Not like a nigger you mean."

"No, I don't mean that."

"You expect me to bluegum it—to say, 'Yessuh, Mr. Bossman, and ain't it been a pleasure and honor for this black trash to lie down and let you all white folks walk over me.'"

"Stop it."

"I went to college," she said.

Earlier he'd found a secondary road into pines, but as he slowed for it he saw a truck parked, blocking the entrance. He drove on.

"I'd like to take you to those places," he said.

"Don't I know."

"Listen, I'm no redneck."

"You're from the land of sky-blue water. I read it on your registration."

"I'd take you to those places if it were possible, but you know it's not."

"Sure I know. I do this all the time."

"I didn't mean that."

"You probably don't even know where to go. Do you know where to go?"

"No."

"You find the dirt roads. You find the shady lanes and bushes where men hide with their women. A lot of hotdogs prefer the fire trails. Just drive on up the highway. I'll show you that too."

He glanced at her but drove on into darkness until she said, "Here." He turned left onto a dirt road under pines. The road crossed a railless wooden bridge. In moon shadows a car was parked.

"We're joining the crowd," she said. "Keep to the left."

The road forked and curved. Bushes brushed the car. "Here," she said. He stopped, thought, and backed in.

"Smart," she said. "You can make a quick getaway."

"Anything wrong with that?"

"But how you know I didn't call some of my soul brothers? How you know they're not hiding in the bushes with their razors ready to jump you when I give the signal?"

He'd already thought of that and wanted to roll up windows and lock doors, yet was afraid she'd resent it.

"I don't know you haven't," he said. He smelled smoke.

"They could be out there right now crawling around the car. You got a fat wallet. They could push the car into the river. Who'd even search for you very long?"

"If you need money, I'll give it to you."

"You mean you want to pay me?"

"I said if you needed money. There's a difference."

"If I need money? Man, man, of course I need money. You think I'd be doing the work I am if I didn't?"

"I'm sorry you have to do that kind of work."

"But if you think I'm going to let you pay me, you're right. Because my cans are empty."

When he said nothing, she laughed.

"He's afraid of me now," she said.

"You really want the money?"

"That's the way the girls do it, isn't it?"

"I don't know how they do it."

"Believe me, it's the way."

He reached for his wallet. She watched him.

"How much?" he asked.

"Surprise me. Show me how much you think I'm worth."

He switched on the dashlight and took a twenty-dollar bill from his wallet. He handed the twenty to her.

"You must think I'm choice meat," she said. "You must think I'm tenderloin."

"Don't talk like that." He switched off the dashlight.

"What's the matter?"   .

"I'm not what you think."

"You think because you helped me put out the fire I owe you something."

"No, and I'd give you more money if I could, but not because of this. Because I like and respect you."

"You got a sweet mouth, honey."

"I wish you wouldn't talk like that."

"All right," she said and pushed the twenty-dollar bill into her uniform pocket. "You tell me what to talk like."

"Right now I don't want you to talk at all."

She leaned forward to untie and remove her tennis shoes, opened the door, and stood barefooted. She unzipped her uniform at the side and pulled it over her head. Carefully she folded it onto the back seat. She reached behind her to unfasten her brassiere and rolled down her white panties. She laid them on her dress. For a moment she merged with the darkness. She stepped into the car, closed the door, and moved across the seat to him.

"Or maybe you'd rather do it on the ground," she said. "You carry a blanket?"

"You're very proficient."

"You want me to get dressed?" She slid away and put a hand on the door latch.

"No."

He reached to her and drew his fingers along her bare arm. He lifted them to her shoulder and neck. She sat without moving, her knees together. Nervous, hot, he drew himself to her and kissed her mouth.

"How is it?" she asked.

"Do you have to keep talking?"

"But you did expect it to be different."

"I don't know what you mean."

"My nigger lips."

"Stop saying those things."

"Isn't it what you were wondering?"

"I told you I'm not like that."

"But didn't you expect it to be a little different?"

"I don't think of you as a Negro."

She laughed and slapped a naked thigh. He pulled his hands away, but she turned to him and put her arms around his neck.

"All right, bossman," she said. "You've paid enough."

During the rest of July and into August he saw her almost every night. When she finished work in the restaurant, she'd walk the road as if on her way home and circle back through the broomstraw to his motel room. He'd have the window up at the rear so she could step in. She materialized from the dark.

At the restaurant he had to act indifferent to her because of Haden, who saw most things. Orson allowed himself to look into her eyes when he ordered, but that was all. One evening when Haden wasn't there, she leaned over the table to write on her order pad. Orson touched her fingers. She withdrew them unhurriedly.

Nights in his room they lay on his bed. The half light cast their dusky shadows on the wall. Sometimes they heard guests in other units. Haden knocked on the door to tell Orson he was wanted on the telephone. Eunice hid in the bathroom. The call was only the mill asking about a misplaced wiring diagram.

Without any discussion Orson had stopped giving her money. Often she stayed the night, and he'd assist her from the window just before dawn. An hour or so later he'd see her working around the kitchen.

"Land of sky-blue water," she said, lying on his bed, her hands over her black breasts. "You going to take me with you when you leave?"

"I'll help you all I can."

"Sure you'll help."

"I mean it. I may be able to get you a job."

"In your house—cleaning, cooking, and carrying out garbage?"

"You shouldn't have to do work of that kind."

The college she'd been to was an all-black institution near Norfolk where she studied history for three semesters.

"In your office maybe?"

"You could go back to school and get your degree. Then you'd be able to teach."

"I'd like to live near a lake—one of those clean northern lakes with spruce trees. They allow us darkies to swim in them, don't they?"

"Stop thinking of yourself in terms of color. Up there you'd be just like everybody else."

"Man, you're dumb. Everybody around here says how smart you are, but you are one dumb John."

By accident he found where she lived. He was driving home from the mill and had to stop for road construction. Among the dusty weeds at the side of the highway was a rural mailbox with Eunice's last name—Riddel—painted aslant it. Black children played around the mailbox and watched the paving machine lay down strips of hot asphalt.

"Does Eunice live there?" Orson called. "Eunice Riddel."

They looked at him. After a moment they nodded. They never did answer, but they kept nodding.

He stared at the house which was little more than a shack—a weathered one-story box set on cinder blocks. The wood had never been painted. The roof was rusty. The front door was open and had no screen. Behind was an outhouse. How did she clean and perfume herself for him?

On a hot Saturday afternoon in August he saw her on the street with a Negro man—a laborer who wore a blue work shirt and filthy overalls. The man was husky and sweaty black. He was powdered by golden dust from a sawmill. Eunice walked obediently behind him.

She didn't come to Orson that night or Sunday either, but on Monday she tapped at his window. He tried not to be angry. He realized he had no justification for anger. Yet he'd begun to believe she belonged to him.

"Don't you think my husband has a right to walk with me on the street?" she asked.

"Your husband?" Slowly Orson sat on the bed.

"You're married. What made you think I wouldn't be?"

He thought of the children in the weeds and of that rough black man having her. He felt sick.

"You want me to leave?" she asked.

She stood in the center of the motel room, still wearing her green uniform. She was both passive and defiant. God, the way she had been used. He was so sorry for her. He stood, crossed to her, and hugged her.

"I was being moral with you," he said. "Self-righteous."

"Don't I know."

"Does your husband know about me?"

"He's not often home."

"Promise if I ever again become righteous you'll call me down."

"I'll whoop and holler," she said.

He was scheduled to finish his work by the middle of September and return to Minnesota. He put off telling Eunice, though he explained his plans to Haden.

"Maybe you'll come back," Haden said.

They were drinking coffee in the restaurant.

"I'd appreciate your not telling anybody I'm leaving."

"Who would I tell?" Haden asked.

Eunice came from the kitchen. She carried a tray of cups which she stacked under the counter.

"You ever met her husband?" Orson asked after she returned to the kitchen.

"Johnny Bell? Sure. He was the prime buck around here for a while. King of the timberhicks. Then he got into trouble. Stole a truck. Cut another nigger too. He was away a while."

"In prison?"

"In prison is right. He was a hotshot with a power saw, but he's trifling now. I expect she's supporting him."

"She looks too nice to have a husband like that."

"Hell you can't figure it about them. I been watching them all my life, and I can't. She looks clean, but I make her get a monthly inspection at the Health Department."

"What sort of inspection?"

"You know—a blood test and smear."

Like cattle, Orson thought. Like herded cattle.

"She's a good worker but hard to get at," Haden said. "In all the time she's been here I never heard her laugh."

"Maybe she hasn't heard anything funny."

"Maybe not." Haden stared. "Why you so concerned?"

"She's a human being I see everyday. I can't help wondering about her."

"Well she probably won't be here much longer. They move on—at least most of them do. You Yankees have made them restless." He smiled to show he was not being unfriendly. "They think salvation's just around the corner."

In the kitchen Eunice dropped something, and it broke.

"You can see she's restless now," Haden said.

Orson had to tell her, but he hated to let go. Her visits through the back window had become a part of him. Wednesday night she lay on the white sheet, her arms at her sides. The light from the lamp laid a sheen on her skin. She lifted a hand to swipe at a fly, and the shadow of the hand crossed the wall.

After he told her, he waited for her to say something. She continued to lie quietly, her eyes open.

"Doesn't it mean anything to you?" he asked.

"Does it mean anything to you?"

"I want to take you out of here."

"To the land of sky-blue water?"

"Anyplace but here."

"Johnny Bell's in jail again."

"Leave him in jail."

"You going to leave your wife for me?"

He didn't speak. She raised her head to look at him.

"Why you think I can do what you can't?" she asked.

"Anything's better than the way you're living."

"Ain't it the truth."

She stood and began to dress. He laid a hand on her warm hip. She stepped away and continued to put on the uniform. In front of the mirror she touched her glossy hair.

"Is there anything I can do for you?" he asked.

"You can give me a hundred dollars. I figure I'm worth that."

He got his checkbook, wrote out the amount, and placed the check on the dressing table. She put the check in her pocketbook.

"Did you care anything for me?" he asked.

"What?"

She was brushing a hand across her stomach, straightening the green uniform, but she turned to look at him.

"Did you come here at all because of me?"

"Or was it the money you mean?"

"I guess I mean that."

"Let me ask you a question. Did you want me because of me? Or do you think you're kind and noble?"

In the half light they stood facing each other. She picked up her pocketbook, walked to the window, and climbed through. She put her head back into the room.

"See you, bossman," she said.

"Don't call me that. I'm not one of them."

"Well think of me in the land of sky-blue," she said.

She was gone into the night, her feet swishing through the broomstraw.

On a sunny September morning he packed his car, shook Haden's hand, and drove the circular drive toward the highway. His radio played. He looked back to the restaurant.

Eunice came from the rear of the kitchen holding a galvanized can. She was burning trash in the wire incinerator. She wore her green uniform and white tennis shoes.

He stopped the car to wave to her. She didn't see him, or pretended not to. Haden spoke to her. She emptied the can, stepped away from the flames, and went inside.

A Walk by the River

Shep unrolled his hammock. The canvas was brown and stiff, each grommet a circle of brass. He tied the nylon lines between two persimmon trees. The bark was deeply grooved, and white blossoms had blown off and lay darkening on rocks and sand.

The trees were not native to West Virginia, but seed had floated up from Virginia and Carolina on the river which flowed north—one of two in the country, he'd read, which did so. Birds and foxes had eaten persimmon fruit dropped near the water's edge and forested the slopes by scattering seed.

He'd packed in along the C&O tracks. The tracks were the only way through the gorge except by the river itself, a route dangerous because of thrashing rapids. The gorge narrowed, and frantic water contorted over rocks and spumed high. Some people challenged the river in kayaks. He and Katie had discovered the gorge on a commercial trip which used a fleet of rubber rafts as large as lifeboats.

He made camp at a place where a stream—Abram's Creek, according to his map—fed into the river. Any water which came off the mountain was pure because the slope was so steep no human could live on it to dirty it. Probably the river itself was okay, but its water was darker, olive colored, and warmer. Drinking from the creeks was better.

There were many of those, falling straight or curving off mountains and smashing white on rocks. Over millenniums the mountains had been undercut by the ancient river, and boulders had either top-pled into it or lodged along the edges. Some boulders resembled herds of elephants come down to drink. They had the same nobility of size and stillness.

He listened to water. The sound was like the sea, and the turbu-lence of rapids caused waves to lap the shore and had created from leached stones a fringe of sandy beach that extended under sycamore and persimmon trees.

Early this morning, after loading his station wagon, he'd left his lifeless apartment and driven south from Charleston to Fayette County for the hike into the gorge. He intended to laze a day or so, at the most two. He would cast a line into the water, but he didn't require fish. The river was enough.

Driftwood was easy to collect, and it looked as it did at the ocean—bleached, ribbed, burnished. Among rocks was wreckage. He found a rusty tire rim. He built a fireplace of stones, and on the stones he set the rim. The holes for the axle and lugs would allow flames through, and the rim furnished a steady surface to boil water.

He lifted a plank which he placed on rocks. Across the plank he laid out equipment. He hung his pack from a stub of broken per-simmon limb. He held his wallet and car keys, looked about, and crossed to a mound of stones under sycamore shade. The stones were shaped like loaves. He hollowed a cache and piled stones over his wallet and keys.

He stripped off his sweaty khakis. Not only sycamores and per-simmons, but also sumac, laurel, and ailanthus shielded him from the railroad tracks on the mountainside. He'd see anybody coming down the river in kayaks or rubber rafts and move into cover before they were close.

He had a swim. The river was almost too warm, carrying the heat of the South, but when he swam close to Abram's Creek the water shriveled him, and the chill stabbed deep into his bones. He let the river drag him downstream. He floated on his back and looked at the orange sky where a scything buzzard wobbled.

He swam to the beach. He collapsed on the sand and slept in the afternoon sun. When he woke and sat up, the sun was behind the mountain. He crawled to the plank for his wristwatch, which he strapped on. It wasn't five o'clock, but the western edge of the gorge was so high that it shadowed the pollen-tinted water. The water had darkened to slate except at rapids where it wanly crashed.

He'd brought a canteen of Cutty Sark. He sat naked on the sand, smoked a cigarette, and drank, using his Sierra cup to mix Scotch with cold, gritty water from Abram's Creek.

He had a sense of being watched. Twice he turned his head, and he slapped at his shoulder, though no fly crossed his skin. He twisted his cigarette into wet sand, stood, and walked to his pack. Up the slope among spiked sumac were two faces. One was a girl's.

He snatched his undershorts from the tree and jerked on his pants. The two faces moved and were masked by sumac. He didn't think the people were gone or he'd have heard the dislodging of stones and the clacking of laurel leaves. He eyed the slope.

They appeared lower, a couple, the young man bearded and wearing bib overalls and a baseball cap. He was tall, and his black hair swung over a long face. His beaded moccasins rasped stones.

The girl was twenty or so, thin, her brown hair collected by a red bandanna tied around her forehead. She wore a denim shirt, Levis, and blackened sneakers. Her face was small, her brown eyes too large. She had to have seen him without clothes.

"We didn't realize anybody was down here," the man said. He raised his chin to clear his face of tangled hair. "We got a camp upstream but need water."

Shep didn't believe it. Anybody knew enough to camp near drinking water. The man carried a dented bucket. He held up the galvanized bucket as if to prove himself.

"There's a snake on the tracks," the girl said. "Copperhead. Pete killed it with a rock."

"I don't go around killing snakes," the man said. "They got as much right to live as anybody, but this one acted like he owned the whole damn C&O."

"I wouldn't have killed it," the girl said.

"You wouldn't walk around it either," the man said. "You were afraid of other snakes in the weeds."

"I would've backed off and given him the tracks," the girl said.

"And gone dry," the man said.

She shrugged and walked to the river's edge where she knelt, stuck lean fingers into sand, and shaped a ball of it.

"Beats Atlantic City," she said.

She tossed the ball of sand into the river. She sat on the plank to unlace and toe off her sneakers. She unbuttoned her shirt and dropped it on the plank. She stepped sideways out of her Levis. She wore nothing except the bandanna which she untied and laid across her shirt. Her brown hair reached her lank buttocks.

She walked into the river and, moving slowly, her arms raised, waded to her hips. She fell forward into the water. She was a clumsy swimmer, lots of splash, little headway. She broke the film of pollen and left a zigzag trail.

The man grinned, worked his black brows, and walked to the creek to fill the bucket. He lifted it, and it leaked. Again he filled it. He pressed a finger against the leak.

"Got a cigarette?" he asked.

Shep almost shook his head, though he knew the man must've seen him smoking earlier. He didn't want the couple around, yet a cigarette had to be given to anybody on the river. He drew the pack from his shirt.

The man took a cigarette. From a slot pocket in the bib overalls he pinched a barn match and struck it by curving a long thumbnail across the head, all the while holding the bucket against his chest and a finger on the leak.

The girl was out in the river. If she swam too far she'd be in the center current which was shoved by rapids. It might capture her. The water didn't appear much faster, but its strength, its grab, was underneath and hidden.

"I never learned how to swim," the man said, words and smoke coming out together.

The girl paddled face upward, the way Shep had, her skin shiny in the slateness of the river. Her breasts flattened above the water. She spouted river. The man whistled, an offkey melody shrilled between teeth. He reached to the plank for the canteen of Scotch, clamped it between his knees, and screwed off the cap. He sniffed and drank.

"Put it down," Shep said.

"Why?" the man asked, again grinning. His large teeth were stained.

"I didn't haul it here for the public."

"But the public likes it," the man said and drank a second time.

"I'm telling you once more to put it down."

"What if I don't wean?"

Shep stared into the murky eyes an instant before walking to the pile of driftwood and lifting a stick big enough to use as a club. He walked back toward the man. The man set the canteen on the plank, the cap still dangling.

"Goddamn neighborly," he said.

The girl called. She was swimming toward shore, but the center current had her. She began to flail water. The man lowered the bucket from his chest, and the leak spurted.

"What should I do?" he asked.

Shep looked at her and at the sweep of the river. He unstrapped his watch and dropped his khakis. He ran. He swerved among rocks and dodged under branches until he was ahead of the girl.

He ran into the river. To intercept, he swam at a slant downstream. She was no longer trying to come in but treading water. When he neared, she kicked feebly and pulled to him.

"Keep swimming," he said.

"Tired," she said.

"Hold me and paddle."

He stroked them toward the shore. In a bow of land was an eddy which would help. The girl breathed hard and glanced at the spray over the rapids. Her hair floated. Her face went under, and he jerked it up.

The center current released them into the curling eddy. He held her as they drifted toward the bank. When his feet touched bottom, he pulled her across in front of him and let her settle in his arms to carry her out. He lowered her to the sand where she folded between her knees.

She gagged, retched, and spat. He looked at the wet lumps of vertebrae along the arch of her back. She crawled to the water and filled a palm to clean her mouth.

"I'll never get the stink of river off me," she said.

He helped her stand. They walked over rocks. She staggered, and he steadied her. Small, thin, weak, she seemed less a woman than a child.

The man was gone. So were the canteen of Scotch and Shep's watch. Equipment was strewed about. The pack of cigarettes had been stolen. Shep crossed to the cache of stones. His wallet and car keys were all right. He peeled down his wet undershorts, pulled on his pants, and shoved the wallet and keys into a pocket.

He looked at the girl. She was buttoning the denim shirt over her wet skin. He remembered the way the man had whistled between his teeth. The whistling could have been a signal. She might've intended only to fake the trouble and gone too far.

"What's his name?" Shep asked.

"Pete Bosley," she said.

"Where's he live?"

"He lives where he is."

"I want more than that," Shep said.

"I don't have more. We just met."

"Where?"

"I was with two other girls, and we had a flat tire near Wheeling. These wild men stopped to help. For a couple of days we convoyed."

"How'd you get here?"

"We stopped at Hawk's Nest, and Pete talked me into hiking to the river with him."

Hawk's Nest was a state park in the forest east of the gorge.

"Did you register at the park?" Shep asked.

"No."

"Where'd you sleep?"

"Pete has an old pickup, but it broke down."

"The license number," Shep said.

"I can't remember the number. Ohio plates. The truck may be

stolen."

He watched her draw her fingers through her hair. He was angry about being robbed, but the worst thing was that maybe there would be no more good days on the river because toughs were taking over the wilderness too.

The man Pete could come back. Shep glanced at the sky. The gorge was already filled with shadow to the brim, yet clouds floated in sunshine. The hike out would be about four hours, part of it in darkness. He had a flashlight or thought he did. He looked in his pack. The flashlight was gone as was his camp knife.

He gathered equipment and fitted it into the pack. He buttoned his own shirt, smoothed his wool socks until they were snug on his feet, and laced his cleated hiking shoes.

"You're coming as far as Thurmond," he said. Thurmond was the railhead where he'd left his station wagon. He'd let the State Police talk to her.

"Not in the dark," she said and hugged herself. "Snakes crawl out on ties at night to get warm."

He hooked his arms through the pack straps. He wouldn't drag her to Thurmond. She'd have to come sometime. The police could wait for her. He started away.

"Don't leave!" she said, hugging herself so hard her shoulders curved inward. "I'm afraid of darkness, and I'll think bears are after me."

She was crying. He again considered the hike to Thurmond. The trestles were dangerous even in daylight. If a snake struck, Shep carried a kit for the bite, though he wasn't certain he'd be able to use it in the blackness of the gorge. He thought of himself down and burning matches over the scalpel and fang holes. He also thought of the man roaming above them on the slope or crouched in wait.

"We'll move upstream," Shep said.

She nodded, wiped her face with the bandanna, and tied it around her neck.

He wound among the boulders. When he glanced behind, he saw the girl was bringing the rusty rim from the fireplace. They ducked sycamore branches, some with leaves stained tan by high water. To complicate their trail, he walked on rocks or waded shallows.

They climbed across slick, rotting logs. Every few hundred yards he stopped to look back and listen. The girl was staggering and breathing through her mouth. At last he found a place which would hide them—a strip of sand between lichen-streaked boulders. He lowered his pack. She dropped the rim, sat, and lay sprawled.

He gathered driftwood. He had no knife to whittle shavings but found boards so dry he could shred them. He laid the fire and lifted the rim the girl had lopsidedly borne. He set it on four stones placed around the flames.

He walked the shore until he found a lard can which he scoured. He filled the can with river water and positioned it on the center of the rim. The girl still lay quietly, though her eyes were open and she stared at the sky.

He kept the fire small to cause a minimum of smoke. When the water steamed, he tore open two packets of bouillon. For himself he had the Sierra cup. For her he found another can, smaller, and used sand a second time to scour. He mixed her bouillon and carried the hot can with his fish pincers.

She held it in both hands, rolling it between her palms and sipping. He drank from his cup. The air of the gorge was cooler, moister. The girl finished quickly and touched her mouth with the back of her fingers.

"I haven't eaten since last night," she said. "Pete bragged we'd live off the land, but he couldn't find anything except some yellow berries which were bitter and probably poison."

Shep had a packet of freeze-dried beef stew which he'd bought by mail from L. L. Bean. He opened it, set the aluminum bag among stones, and poured in hot water. He let the stew steep.

He filled her can and his cup. They drank the stew. In the dusk the rapids sounded louder. Smoke from his fire slid out over water and formed a low, shifting layer. He made coffee, using instant he'd brought along in an envelope. He washed her can and poured.

She drew a finger along the edge of her hair. The hair was dry. Now that she was fed and composed, she was softer, her shoulders more rounded. All of her had become more rounded, as if her bones had drawn in. She was almost attractive in a ratty fashion. He imagined her in a dress and nylons. She could be stylish with her

undernourished face and angularity. He didn't trust her, but he
appreciated the way she'd carried the rim.

"I thought it'd be paradise away from home and free," she said.
"Instead I've been hungry for a month. I don't even own a cake of
soap."

He drank his coffee and didn't speak.

"Course the river washed me pretty good," she said. "I still have
the taste of drowning in my mouth."

He knew she was trying to force him to talk, but he looked at the
river.

"You always go places alone?" she asked, turning her knees
toward him.

"If I can," he said.

He was credit manager of a department store. When he didn't
have to think about the job, he liked the work, if that made sense.
He got involved in the numbers.

Katie had been his wife for almost eight years. One winter evening
he came back from the store to their house, and she was gone. She
had taken some jewelry and clothes, but there was no note, no word
for him. The police couldn't find her. For months he'd heard
nothing.

Then he received a letter from an attorney in Tyler, Texas. Katie
wanted a divorce. Shep finally located her by phone. She said she
intended to marry an engineer from Union Carbide, a friend Shep
had played tennis with weekly until the man was transferred from
Charleston.

"I betrayed you," she said.

"Betrayed?" Shep asked. "Betrayed!"

"I like and respect you as much as anybody I've ever known, but it
was never love," she said. "Please forgive me."

"What the hell was it if it wasn't love?" Shep shouted.

The darkness of the gorge was blacker than the sky. No stars
shone, though the clouds lacked the loom of rain. The river was a
faint slickness except at the rapids where it broke a fleeting white.
He unrolled the space blanket he used as a ground cover or as a
poncho in rain. The girl slapped at a mosquito. He found the can

of insect repellent and strung the hammock.

"You can have it or the blanket," he said.

"I don't like high places," she said.

"Girls go upstream, boys down," he said.

He walked downstream until he couldn't see the fire. When he went back, she came from under a sycamore. She hadn't gone too far from the light. He threw sand on the fire.

He took off his shoes before balancing in the hammock. As a weapon he held a rock. He heard her lie and change positions on the space blanket. He also heard the river, the sizzling of embers, and a train whose clanking above them merged with the wash of the rapids.

He couldn't sleep. He imagined the man stalking them in darkness. Maybe the girl was just waiting. He sat up.

"You're worried he'll come back," she said.

"That's one worry," Shep said.

"You mean me," she said.

He didn't answer.

"I'll admit to helping him," she said. "We were out of money, and the truck broke. He told me if we could steal our way to North Carolina he had a brother who'd take us in. But I nearly drowned. He didn't care I nearly drowned."

"What would you guess he's doing now?" Shep asked.

"If there's enough firewater in your canteen, he's wallowing," she said.

Shep lay back. He still held the rock. The hammock swung slightly. He listened to the rapids. He felt himself sinking, and the river seemed to be in the hammock with him, the noise of the flow. He had the sensation of weltering in a pool of dark water.

When he woke, he believed he was being attacked. The girl was over him.

"It can't be done," she said. She was naked, and her gamy hair dropped around his face. "Hammock mechanics make it impossible."

Astride him, she was unbuttoning his shirt. He attempted to stop the rolling of the hammock. She shifted her knees, and the hammock spun.

Together they hit. On either side of them were rocks, but it was on sand they landed. For a moment they sat jarred. She felt for him and pulled at his clothes.

She was the first woman since Katie. For a long time he hadn't wanted anyone, and then he'd become uncertain he could handle a woman ever again, but with this slight girl he was repaired. He kissed her face and hair, wanting to forget, and almost able to, that she was hippie trash.

During the night he roused her. The moon was uncovered and bright enough to cause sycamores to shade the boulders. She set her feet against going into the water with him, but he tightened his hand on her wrist and led her. Chilled they lay wet body to body under the folded space blanket. She smelled of river.

She was up in the morning before him. He raised on an elbow. The fire burned, and the lard can steamed. She had dressed.

"I found Tang in your pack," she said.

She brought him Tang mixed in his Sierra cup. She then used the cup to cook freeze-dried scrambled eggs. The eggs had bits of cheese in them. He sat by her on the sand to drink coffee. The gorge was misty, but the sun was up there, and the mist would burn away to a clean morning.

"Can we stay a little longer?" she asked as he unstrung the hammock.

"I could fish an hour," he said. "We'd still hike out by noon."

He wore his damp undershorts and laced on the tennis shoes he used for wading. He had a telescopic rod. He fastened a plug to the bronze swivel of his line, a humpbacked green-and-white bass slayer. He moved upstream in shallows to cast along the bank and under sycamores. She stayed on the sand, her arms around her knees, her face lifted.

The fish struck in smooth water on the downstream side of a boulder. Shep believed it was a smallmouth, but the fish didn't surface when he checked it, and the pull was erratic. It had to be a channel cat.

The channel cat was no passive brooding citizen of the river's deep holes like its mudcat cousin. It was a game fish which possessed heart and power. If Shep could beach it, he'd fillet it, wrap it in aluminum foil, and souse it with tube butter. He'd bury the fillets under an inch or so of sand and rake coals from the fire over the sand. In twenty minutes the chunky white catfish meat would be savory hot on the tongue. He remembered he didn't have a knife, but there was the tiny scalpel in the snake-bite kit.

The angles of the monofilament line increased as the fish swam deeper. Shep glanced behind him to call the girl so she could watch. She stood by the river, and with her was the man. Shep allowed the rod to slacken. The fish spat out the plug, and the line became limp.

Shep ran through water and along the bank. A branch slashed him. The plug snagged driftwood, and the line snapped across his face. He dropped the rod. A foot sank into muck and threw him. Up again, he ran. He scooped a rock from the shore.

The man flung Shep's pants to the ground. He'd taken the car keys and wallet and was pocketing them. Around his neck were several pairs of hiking boots tied by their laces. He wore Shep's canteen and wrist watch. From the overalls he yanked a .22 caliber target pistol. He held it with both hands and aimed it at Shep's face. Shep let the rock fall.

"What was you thinking of doing?" the man asked.

"Where'd you get the gun?" the girl asked.

"Same place I got the boots," he said. "Three fishing dudes back there are going to have a long walk barefooted. Slept too late. And look what else."

From a hip pocket he drew wallets, four of them counting Shep's. He opened each to show money. He laughed and flapped the wallets at the girl.

"Leave me my cards and driver's license," Shep said.

"Oh naw," the man said. "We going to use the cards and the car. Now where's it parked?"

Shep didn't answer. The girl stood watching.

"Don't tell us you done forgot how to make words," the man said, pushing the wallets into the hip pocket.

When the .22 dipped, Shep lunged. He heard the girl's cry. The gun hit him in the mouth. He was knocked sideways and to a knee. He choked on blood.

"Hero," the man said. "Now where's the goddamn car?"

Holding a hand to his bleeding mouth, Shep looked to the girl. Her expression showed nothing. The man moved toward Shep and raised the gun to hit again.

"It's at Thurmond," the girl said.

"Where in Thurmond?"

Shep didn't answer. The man again raised the gun.

"Don't be dumb," the girl said. "Tell him."

"Next to the station," Shep said, an arm over his head.

"Make and model," the man said, the gun still raised.

"Seventy-six Chevy station wagon," Shep said.

"Now take off your tennis shoes," the man said.

Shep untied them. The man pitched them into the river. He stooped, backed off, and strung Shep's hiking shoes around his neck with the stolen boots.

"You go on and fish," the man said. "You catch a fish and eat it or you got some food left, but don't follow us until tomorrow. The insurance companies pay for everything, or almost everything, so enjoy."

The girl was knotting the bandanna around her forehead.

"To make sure you don't birddog us, we might stop along the tracks somewhere," the man said. "Might be in the weeds or hiding behind a tree. If you come, we go bang, bang, bang, bang. We could be behind any bush."

Shep no longer looked toward the girl.

The man and she climbed the slope. Their feet left a trail in the moisture. The girl never glanced back. Laurel closed around them.

Shep didn't fish. His head ached. He patted water on his torn lip and lay by the river. When the sun was straight up, he collected equipment, shouldered his pack, and hiked to the tracks. He doubted the man and the girl were still in the gorge. Shep could be out by late afternoon.

Sharp rock ballast forced him to shortstep it on the ties. During the first mile his socks wore off. Jagged creosote punctured his feet.

The feet began to bleed. He stopped to draw out splinters.

The farther he went, the less he worried about the man and girl. By now they were on the road to North Carolina if the girl had told Shep any truth, which she probably hadn't. He wouldn't think of her.

He stopped at a stream flowing under the tracks and soaked his feet in the numbing water. Again he hiked on ties. A clanging freight train came fast, and he tried to wave it down, but it rolled on, the engineer gazing like God, and Shep tottered on bleeding feet among dusty sumac.

Each step against the ties jabbed pain into him. His toes drew stiffly upward, and he limped on the sides of his feet. He no longer searched the tracks ahead but trudged bowed, his eyes blurred, his arms dangling. Sweat fell into cinders. He let his pack slide free. Shadow rose on the slope below, and when the shadow touched him he felt its blessed coolness.

He was almost on the girl before he saw her. She sat in flattened weeds beside the tracks, her legs outspread, her hands behind to prop her. Angrily he tilted toward her.

He stopped before reaching her. Her face was bruised, her left eye battered nearly shut. Her bleeding nose had caked. Her shoes too were gone, and her feet blackened and galled. Blood prints on the ties, hers, led toward him, not Thurmond. She had been coming back.

"Throw you away, did he?" Shep asked.

"I went to take him off you," she said, her voice a whisper.

"You yipped when I tried for his gun," Shep said.

"Because I was afraid for you," she said. She closed her eyes and let her head loll forward as if to sleep.

He considered. It made a kind of sense, but odds were long as the old river she was lying, hell yes. Yet maybe not. He was in no condition to weigh the truth.

Neither could he leave her nor any of the world's wounded to loneliness, grief, and fear of darkness. He roused her to a wobbly stand among the weeds. Together, bumping hip and thigh, they wove their way between the shadowed tracks.

Sea Treader

I was caulking a skiff the first time Mr. E. B. Freestone came down to the river—a Virginia tidal river so wide you couldn't see the other shore. The water was salty enough to keep us who went swimming in it from catching poison ivy, though the salt didn't help with chiggers and ticks that dropped on us from the drooping pines. The river, named by Indians the Bromanni, emptied into the Chesapeake Bay a few miles below the landing. Farther south—south by east to be exact—the bay flowed into the Atlantic Ocean.

Mr. E. B. Freestone arrived in a blue Buick, a car with no scratches or dents, but old. The hot metal was dusty from the ride across the greening marshes to the landing. The wharf, built on creosoted pilings, belonged to Mr. Henry Peters. Watermen docked alongside. A few pleasure boats weltered in berths, boats owned by city people. There were no fancy ones.

Big Orange and Honest Snuff signs splotched Mr. Peters's store above the landing, an unpainted frame building with a red tin roof. Up the river was a tomato cannery that was used in July and August. The long shed had open sides and aluminum sinks where women— black and white—worked. They wore bright kerchiefs around their heads. Their fingers became so skilled with knives they sliced instinctively, the blades quickly looping into the pulp. Women's talk and laughter carried a long way across the hot still water of summer.

Beyond the cannery and near the pines was what was left of an oyster-shucking house. It had gone out of business. The walls of the house were a weather-polished gray, and leaning. On the bank were piles of shells, the insides bone white and reflecting sun.

I worked for Mr. Henry Peters all day during summers and part time when school was open. I pumped gas, cut bait, and repaired boats. Mr. Peters was an elderly white-haired man given to sitting on his store porch with his hands folded over his stomach, chewing and spitting into the sand. Occasionally he stirred enough to go out in his powerboat with me to catch croakers or dip for crabs in the warm shallow water of coves along the river.

The afternoon Mr. E. B. Freestone arrived in his old Buick, I was the only person at the landing. Mr. Peters had gone to Norfolk for a funeral—his sister's husband had died of shaking palsy—and he'd worn his dark suit and hat. Before driving off, he'd left the keys to the store with me.

"No credit," he said. "On anything, including gas."

He disbelieved in credit because he'd lost his trucking business during the Depression. Now we figured he buried his money in tomato cans. He could have made a lot more by building a modern marina with lights and a restaurant, but he no longer trusted bankers or mankind. Any day he expected another crash, and he sat on his store porch and squinted across the water as if listening for the first rumble.

I heard the Buick before I saw it—coming down a road which was white with crushed shells. The shells crackled under the tires. Dust spun and rose. We'd had a hot spring with little rain, and the river and bay were glazed. Heat shimmered up, bending vision. Jellyfish had floated in early and washed to the store, where they dried into little bits of fluff. In the water they could be large, with streamers three or four feet long, but on shore they became small strings of fluff that the breeze blew away.

Mr. Freestone stopped his Buick in front of the store. He got out, looked around, and climbed the steps to the porch. He tried the door. He shaded his eyes to peer through the glass, then stood indecisively until he heard the tap of my mallet. He stared a moment and walked down the steps and crossed among boats to the edge of the water.

"Do you run the store?" he asked.

"Sometimes."

Mr. Freestone was a small man, very clean, with a red com-
plexion and soft white hands. He appeared dapper in white slacks,
a blue linen blazer with brass buttons, and one of those billed yachting caps that city sailors wear. His black-and-white shoes had per-
forated toes.

"What about now?" he asked. "Do you run it now?" He smiled.
"I'm almost out of gas."

"We don't take credit cards," I said. He had gray hair and a
small, precisely trimmed gray moustache. He stroked the moustache
as if soothing it. He'd been drinking and was unsteady.

"Well if you'll take dollar bills, I'll pay," he said.

I didn't hurry. I finished the seam. On the river we knew about
tourists. They came for a while. They bought boats to drink on, and
their beer cans floated into our tidal creeks. They might be enthusiastic for a summer or two, but eventually they left and their boats
passed into other hands or became skeletons on our shores.

I walked him up the landing, unlocked the store, and switched on
the electricity which operated the gasoline pump. I filled the tank of
his Buick. He paid me with a twenty-dollar bill. I carried it into the
store to make change. He followed and picked up two twenty-cent
cigars.

"Take these out," he said, showing me the cigars. He crossed to
the cooler. "Join me in a Sunrise?"

"No," I said. My fingers were on the cash register, ready to punch
when he had everything.

"Well I'll drink one," he said.

"You going to take the bottle?"

"I'll drink it here." He smiled. "If you don't mind."

I laid his change on the counter and waited while he drank. He
stuck the bottle into the crate. As soon as he was on the porch, I
locked the door and walked back to the skiff.

He followed, stood on the wharf, and unwrapped a cigar.

"Okay for me to smoke here?" he asked.

"Try not to burn us out," I said.

I started caulking another seam, placing oakum along the joint and tapping it in. He struck a match, puffed, and blew out the flame. He flapped his hands behind him and rose on his toes.

"I envy the way you do that," he said. "I always wanted to work with my hands and teach my son to work with his."

I went on caulking. I was used to drinkers. He smoked and stared across the water.

"How far is it to the ocean?" he asked.

"Twenty-seven miles." I'd been there with my father in his boat the day before he died.

"I feel this crazy desire to see the ocean." He puffed on the cigar, coughed, and patted his chest. "I've never been on the water. I've been in a rowboat on a pond, but never the big water."

I looked at him and at his yachting cap with the captain's insignia of two crossed golden anchors.

"Oh I see," he said. He took off the cap and examined the insignia. "Bad form, huh? To wear this?"

I shrugged.

"Well I didn't know," he said. "I stopped at a store. They had these caps in the window." He held the cap. "If it offends you, I won't wear it."

I eyed him. What the hell did I care if he wore it or not. I continued caulking. He shaded his eyes. The afternoon heat was more stinging than the flies. Dusty pines lowered boughs as if exhausted. Gulls quieted and settled to the water.

"I've been thinking of buying a boat," he said. "Boats have been running in my mind.

I tapped and wiped sweat from my face.

"Not that I'm rich. I couldn't afford a cabin cruiser. But I thought perhaps a sailboat—a small craft rigged for one person to handle. Is such a buy possible?"

"Do you want an engine in her?" I asked.

"How do you feel about engines?"

"If you're a real sailor, you shouldn't need one," I said. It was what my father had believed. For years he'd worked oyster beds by wind alone. I'd seen him looking like a Viking and riding his skip-jack on the flashing foam of black winter waves pushing in from the sea.

"Well I want to be a real sailor," he said. He still held his cap. "Do you know of any boats?"

"You can drive in any direction and find dealers."

"The problem is I'm ignorant about boats. I need an advisor." He smiled. "I'd be glad to pay you for your time."

I lowered my mallet. I knew about boats all right. I'd practically been born in one, and my father had died in a nor'easter before he was thirty. I saw a chance to make some money. Tourists were fair game, and there was a season on them just like ducks and geese. You took it off them when you could.

"I can't do anything until I finish work," I said.

"That's perfectly all right. I'm in no hurry whatsoever. By the way, my name is Freestone—E. B. Freestone."

"Mine's Benson. Billy Benson."

"Well I'll just wait around and smoke until you're through."

At five-thirty Mr. Henry Peters came back from the funeral. He walked down to the wharf to get the keys to the store. Mr. Freestone stood from a bollard and introduced himself. Mr. Peters shook Mr. Freestone's hand and looked at him as if he were a piece of meat on the scale.

"I don't extend no credit," Mr. Peters said. The dark hat he'd been wearing had left a red welt around his sweaty forehead, and his white hair was pasted in ringlets against his skin.

"I don't blame you," Mr. Freestone said. "You can sleep nights."

"Sometimes I sleep days too," Mr. Peters said. He went up to the store.

I put away tools, washed my hands under a faucet, and buttoned my khaki shirt. Mr. Freestone waited for me in his Buick.

We drove the shoreline. I found him half a dozen boats, good stout twenties built right there on the river, but though he was polite, he shook his head.

"Don't you know of anything else?" he asked.

"Maybe you better tell me more about what you want," I said. I smelled the sour liquor on him.

"Here," he said and pulled an Exxon map from his glove compartment. His fingers were shaky, but with his pencil he drew a neat sketch on the blue Chesapeake Bay. "Something like this."

What he had in mind was a racing sloop, narrow of beam, bold of bow. She needed to be trimmer, more dashing, than our local boats. I didn't know of any like it for sale, but I knew of a poor imitation which could be had. Mr. Ed Shin, a lawyer, had bought the boat for his daughter Mary. Now she'd left home and was rearing a family in Baltimore. The *Bonnie Mary,* moored to a stake, swung neglected with the wind.

Mr. Freestone and I stood on the lawn in front of Mr. Shin's house and looked at her. Half submerged, she shifted listlessly, nudged by the tide. She was built before fiberglass. Mr. Freestone walked up and down the bank.

"Can we go out there?" he asked.

I went to the house and got permission from the maid to use the skiff. We rowed out. The sun was just lowering into the slack water and gilding it. Mr. Freestone sat in the exact center of the stern, his small white hands on his knees. His gray eyes were excited. We drew alongside the *Bonnie Mary.* Slatted floorboards floated in the cockpit. The tiller bumped a bulkhead.

"I'm interested," he said. He kept touching the gunwales. Perhaps in the evening glare he couldn't see clearly. "If the price is right." He turned to me. "The price has to be right. Do you think you can get her?"

"It'll take some talking," I lied.

"You do the talking—and if the price is right, I'll give you a commission," he said.

I rowed him back to the slip. He drove me home. He would, he explained, return the next weekend. Negotiations he left to me.

"And I know you'll get her," he said.

I stood in front of my house—a white clapboard cottage among the pines—and watched Mr. Freestone drive into darkness.

"Who was that?" my mother asked through the screen door. She was still a young woman. Her eyes and hair were black, but she was pale and often weary. She worked at the cannery when it was operating and at the farm co-op the rest of the year.

"Easy pickings," I said.

"Well you come in and eat." She wore an apron over her pink dress. On her feet were furry bedroom slippers—once white but now smudged. She pushed at her hair with the back of her hand and sighed.

She was going out with a waterman who'd been a friend of my father. I'd sat in a movie one night and heard her laughing. The laughter was strange because I thought of her bending over a coffin, her black hair tangled, her face wet. Later the same night as the movie I saw her on the street with the waterman, her hand on his arm. My expression when we passed startled her. After she came home, she sat on the edge of my bed.

"I'm lonely sometimes," she said. In the darkness she touched my face. "You don't know about that yet. All lonely people deserve forgiveness."

And she cried.

I went to see Mr. Shin on Saturday morning. He sat at a white metal table on his front lawn. A yellow umbrella stuck out of the center of the table. His checkered shirt was open at the collar, and he was eating grapefruit. He had a pocked face and blond wavy hair.

"What makes you think I want to sell?" he asked. He narrowed his reddish-brown eyes as if taking aim.

"You don't even bail her," I said.

"But I can bail her if I want to."

"Well do you want to?"

"How much you offering?"

"I'm acting for somebody else."

"Who?"

"A fellow I know."

"I assume you know him if you're buying him a boat. Does he live around here?"

"Not right around here."

"Ah," Shin said and smiled. He couldn't be fooled. He made his living skinning people. "If he's meat, I get a better price."

I didn't say anything. I intended to get part of the price myself, plus the commission.

"Tell you what," Shin said. He scratched his neck. "I'd like to have three thousand for her." He smiled. "You can keep anything she brings over that."

"Thanks a whole bunch," I said. I didn't like being seen through by Shin, plus the boat wasn't worth the price, and I didn't believe Mr. Freestone would go for the deal.

When he arrived Sunday afternoon, I was at the landing. He drove his dusty Buick and wore a gray business suit and yellowed Panama hat. His face was sweaty red. I couldn't tell whether or not he'd been drinking, but he was anxious.

"I should have asked you to get in touch," he said. "I tried to call you, but there's no phone listed."

"There's no phone to be listed," I said.

"Well?" he asked. He shifted from foot to foot.

"Shin wants three thousand one," I said, adding the extra hundred. I didn't exactly look at Mr. Freestone. Instead I sorted peeler crabs in the bait box.

"Oh." Slowly he sat on the bollard. He wiped his face with his handerchief. "That's steeper than I expected."

"Best I could do," I said. "He doesn't have to sell."

"Do you think it's a fair price?"

"If you're happy with what you get, it's a fair price," I said, avoiding his eyes. He will, I thought, go to Shin and find the truth. Somehow I'll be done out of the money—if there is any money.

"Let's see," Mr. Freestone said. He took a pencil and envelope from his inside coat pocket. He wrote figures and looked at them doubtfully.

"There'll be a commission for you," he said. "Is five percent. enough?"

"Whatever you think's right," I said. The commission was three times what I'd allowed myself to hope for.

"That's another hundred and fifty-five," he said. He figured, blew out his cheeks, and put away the pencil and envelope. "At my age what's a few hundred? While I'm trying to horsetrade Mr. Shin, somebody else might buy *Sea Treader.*"

"Buy who?" I asked.

"*Sea Treader.* It's the name I decided on. I have a right to name her, don't I?"

"When she's yours, you're the master."

"Then master I'll be. You close the deal." He wrote the check on a Richmond bank, folded it once, and handed it to me. "Also bring her over and dock her."

"I'll have to pump her out. And she'll need lots of work before she's seaworthy."

"Seaworthy. To be worthy of the sea. Well I want you to do it. And, of course, you'll be compensated. Now I need a couple of cigars to get me back to the city."

The same evening I carried the check to Mr. Shin. He said he'd put it in the bank and allow a few days for it to clear. The idea made me nervous. I saw the money taking wing. In my sleep I actually saw it flying away through the clouds. So on Wednesday I went to see him again and stood around on his porch until he wrote me a check for a hundred dollars.

I then pumped the boat, unfurled the aging sail, and ran it up the mast. Shin, who'd rowed me out, watched from his skiff.

"You got a good thing going," he said.

"If I don't sink first."

Even pumped she was heavy. Some of her timbers were water-logged, and there was a leak in her starboard quarter. The sails were gray and molding. Stitches had pulled loose. She mushed to tiller. I had to keep bailing. I felt ashamed.

I sailed her around the point and into Mr. Peters's landing where I beached her. Amos White, a colored oysterman, helped me lay rails. We struck her canvas and mast, used a hand winch to pull her onto the rails, and braced her.

"She's sick," Amos said. His skin as black as caulking tar, he was bent but strong. He wore a baseball cap, overalls, and rubber boots. "She needs medicine."

"Don't I know it."

"He'd be better off putting his money back in the bank."

"I know that too."

But when Mr. Freestone came the next Saturday he was pleased. He happily paid me my hundred-and-fifty-five-dollar commission and ten more for bringing her around the point. Just the idea of owning a boat thrilled him. He kept circling her, his small feet almost dancing. He reached up and touched her name—*Bonnie Mary*—on the transom.

"We'll soon have that off," he said. "No disrespect intended to the lady." He faced me. "I want you to keep working."

"I'll work when I can."

"How much do you get an hour?"

"Three fifty," I lied. His was a stupid question. I got what I could. "And I'll have to buy materials."

"You're hired."

Most days after I finished for Mr. Peters, I was able to work on the boat. I scraped her bottom, replaced a rib and two timbers, patched the leak, and caulked her. I sanded her and put on two coats of fiberglass.

Mr. Peters occasionally walked down from the store to watch. He wore a tan fishing hat that had a green visor sewed into the brim. His old face, like a turtle's, only stubbled with beard, expressed doubt.

"You know anything about him?" he asked of Mr. Freestone.

"Only that his checks are good," I said.

"That's right much," Mr. Peters said. He rocked on his squeaky black shoes and clinked coins in his pocket. "He don't know what he's doing, does he?"

"Nope."

"There's nothing as helpless as a tourist," Mr. Peters said.

Mr. Freestone was eager to work with me on *Sea Treader,* but he was a mess. What little jobs I gave him he did wrong, and I'd have to correct them. I shouldn't have cared. It was his three fifty an hour. But it was exasperating to have to rewire the battery-powered running lights or find he'd failed to use brass screws in the fairleads.

"I find great satisfaction working with my hands," he said. He twisted a turnbuckle in the wrong direction. "I should have learned a trade."

"The other way," I told him about the turnbuckle. He was supposed to be tightening the headstay.

"Oh." He smiled and reversed those small white hands. "Imagine being a shipbuilder. Now that would furnish a man pride. He could walk up to the King of England, look him in the eye, and say, 'Sir, I build ships.'"

"What kind of work do you do?" I asked and pretended to be busy with the rudder I was mounting.

"Why I count the bloody nuts," he said. He smiled and walked to his car.

He was often a little tight. He'd stroll to his Buick and duck to lift the bottle from the floor—usually a pint of bourbon in a brown paper bag. He'd glance about and duck a second time to drink.

When he came the next weekend he brought three boxes of candy with him. Each contained twenty-four bars of a confection named Virginia Divinity. He gave a box to Mr. Peters, a box to me, and said I could give the third box to my girl, which I did. Every week after that he had candy with him.

Actually Virginia Divinity wasn't so bad. The bars were maybe a little too sweet. Once in a while a bite would set my teeth on edge. It was the kind of candy I might not pay money for, but that I didn't mind eating when nothing else was around.

I was ready to fit *Sea Treader* with new sails. Mr. Freestone became really excited. I felt I was older than he was. He circled, crawled under her, and stroked the repaired centerboard housing. He polished fittings with his handerchief and fingered canvas. He urged me to paint her name on the transom. I did, and he looked over my shoulder, his bourbon breath warm on my neck.

He bought champagne for a christening but then didn't want to hit the bottle against the newly varnished bowsprit. Instead he smashed the champagne on the anchor. He and I pushed the boat into the water. Mr. Peters and Amos White stood by. Mr. Freestone gave out cigars and offered Mr. Peters and Amos a drink.

I moored *Sea Treader* to a stake. Mr. Freestone rose in the skiff and proposed a toast. He dipped his pint toward her. "May she find

a port worthy of her beauty and an ocean deserving of her grace."
He drank. "You'll have to teach me to sail. And I'll pay you for it."

I thought I heard something in his voice, but he lifted the pint and
laughed across the water.

As a sailor he didn't know windward from leeward or a sheet from
a halyard. I'd go out with him in the late afternoon. I sat him at the
tiller while I minded the jib and main.

"I want to learn that too," he said, fidgeting, his hands anxious to
reach everything.

"You learn to hold a course first. Look at your wake."

He turned and saw bubbles rising from under *Sea Treader*. They
snaked away on grayish-blue water, but he was still enthusiastic.

"To be moved by wind—the same wind perhaps that sped Ulysses
onward. You ever think of that? We might have the same wind in
these sails that sped Ulysses."

I told him I'd never thought of it.

"I didn't realize sailing would be so noisy," he said. He was
speaking of the drag of the boat through the water and the slap of
waves against the bow. "The sea actually talks."

I worked him sailing close-hauled, reaching, and running before
the wind. I taught him to come about and jibe. When he wasn't looking, I'd drop a plank overboard and make him tack to it. We prac-
ticed swinging upwind into moorings.

A squall caught us in the bay. Seething black clouds tumbled over
us. The water too became black, fringed with the white of hissing
foam. Rain slanted into our faces.

I let him handle *Sea Treader* alone. He lowered his mainsail and
we swept along on the jib. Rain popped against our slickers. Wind
buffeted us, and water stung our eyes, but as we shot across the jagged water he was happy and excited. When the boat planed, he
called into the wind.

Later the sun came out, and the air became warm and bluish. He
hated to return to the landing. I told him I had a date. Reluctantly
he swung the tiller.

"Lord that was fine, wasn't it?" he asked. He looked at the
washed sky. "I wish Betts could've seen me do that."

"Who's Betts?"

Glancing at me, he took off his yellow slicker and stowed it in the cabin.

"My wife."

We moored, furled the sails loosely so they would dry, and climbed into the skiff. He liked to row.

"She never saw me do anything swashbuckling," he said. He pulled us toward the wharf. "Did you ever read *Captain Blood*?"

"No."

"It's one of the great books. Written by an author named Sabatini. As a boy I read it a hundred times. I saw the movie every day for a week. In my dreams I swung from the shrouds with a cutlass in my teeth. That's what I mean by swashbuckling."

"Is she dead?"

"Who?"

"Your wife."

"Not technically."

He hadn't yet been out to sail by himself, and he was nervous about it. I waited for a quiet afternoon with an offshore breeze. When he climbed aboard *Sea Treader*, I stayed in the skiff. For a moment he was afraid.

"You really think I can do this?" he asked.

"On your back you can do it," I said.

"All right," he said but frowned. "It shouldn't be any different without you."

"It's easier because nobody's in your way," I said.

Acting determined, he hoisted his mainsail and jib, stuck in the tiller, and cast off. I rowed back to the landing and watched. Mr. Peters came out.

Mr. Freestone tacked to the black buoy and jibed around it. He stayed just short of the bay. He came in fast, the breeze behind him.

"I reckon he won't drown himself," Mr. Peters said. He went back into the store.

I rowed the skiff across the water. Mr. Freestone had made *Sea Treader* secure and was snapping his fingers.

"You see me jibe that buoy?" he called.

"You should never jibe unless you have to," I said.

"But I did it with class, didn't I?" he asked and laughed. "Swashbuckling."

He reached across the gunwale and shook my hand.

At the end of summer I thought he'd want me to outhaul his boat, but he kept coming on weekends. He'd drive in on Saturday and stay over at a small motel on the coast. Occasionally he'd arrive during the week. He sailed farther and farther into the bay. He carried a hamper with him and always his bottle.

"I'd like to take a long trip," he said.

"Your boat isn't built for long trips," I said.

"Men in smaller boats have crossed the sea."

"They've died too."

"It's a fact." He looked toward the bay. "How far did you say it was to the ocean?"

"You don't want to go there."

"You're absolutely right. I don't want to."

But he went one Sunday morning early, before I reached the landing. He didn't return until almost dark. His face was flushed. He'd sailed as far as the Chesapeake Bay Bridge Tunnel and seen a freighter moving along the Baltimore channel and out to sea.

"It was glorious!" he said. "Big birds were soaring. The swells were long and deep. And the sun was drawing up water."

"You're lucky you got back," I said.

"I've always been lucky," he said.

The autumn came slowly. It was the best time of year on the shore. Jellyfish were gone, the days were warm, and the lapping of the water slowed. At night, coolness settled on the bay and quieted the land.

I was dating a girl named Laura Lee. I had a car, a second-hand Chevrolet I'd bought with money I made off Mr. Freestone. Laura Lee and I would park by the river and watch the lights on passing boats. She was a brunette, a big girl who played basketball, yet womanly. She wore sandals, jeans, and a yellow basketball jersey.

"I'm almost out of candy again," she said. She was combing her hair. "Can you get me another box off Mr. Freestone?"

"You ever consider buying some for yourself?" I asked. I adjusted the radio.

She stared. "And why are you being so mean-mouthed to me?"

"Me?"

"But definitely you."

I guess the reason was Mr. Freestone kept paying me. I didn't ask for it, yet he always handed me money for helping him. If I tried to refuse, he'd stuff a couple of dollars into my shirt pocket.

"You paid me enough already," I told him one afternoon after splicing some lines for him. "I don't want money for everything."

He was surprised and took back his hand.

"You give it away too easily," I explained. "Hell, a baby could get it off you."

And the damnedest thing happened. I found myself confessing. I couldn't look at him. I talked my words into the wharf. He stood listening. "I got not only your commission," I said. "I added another hundred to Mr. Shin's price."

He didn't speak. I heard the gulls squeaking and squawking. Slowly he smiled.

"I'm not a complete idiot," he said. "Anyway you haven't told me anything I didn't know."

"Huh?"

"Mr. Shin telephoned me in Richmond and wanted to deal directly. He would've cut you out."

That bastard Shin! I was still so mad that evening I started for his house. I would've gone except Laura Lee stopped me. She held me around the waist. Later, still shamed, I offered to give the hundred back to Mr. Freestone—in installments.

"I don't want it back," he said and touched my arm. "Even at the price you're cheap. Look what a sailor you've turned me into."

"You know what I think?" Laura Lee asked when I parked on the point and we watched the lights of a yacht slide across the black bay. "I think Mr. Freestone's sweeter than Virginia Divinity."

That same warm October weekend we had a visitor. While Mr. Freestone was readying his gear for a sail, a car came fast down the road. Shells cracked under the tires and pinged against the frame. It was a red Lincoln with a white top. The driver was a stocky young man with black curly hair. He wore a purple shirt and slacks. On his feet were clogs which banged against the wharf.

"This where you've been hiding?" he asked.

"Who's been hiding?" Mr. Freestone answered and kept loading the skiff.

"Well I have to talk to you."

"And I have to go sailing."

"Is that the boat?" the young man asked. He looked at *Sea Treader*. He took off his sunglasses to look at her. "I expected the *Queen Elizabeth II*."

"You don't know anything," Mr. Freestone said. He turned to me. I was stirring bait. "He plays golf."

"Come to the car and let's talk," the young man said.

"You can talk here," Mr. Freestone said. "This is Billy Benson, and he's seen me under the stress of a storm. He's seen me flying on my jib." Again he turned to me. "He's a real estate entrepreneur, a very big deal."

"All right," the young man said.

"A very, very big deal. Of course he has an in. He married the boss's daughter."

"What's the good in this?" the young man asked.

"There's no good in it, and I'm going sailing," Mr. Freestone said. He climbed into the skiff.

"You got Mom worried. She keeps phoning me."

"Well you comfort her. Tell her I've become a swashbuckler."

"What about your job? They're phoning too."

"They can't make Virginia Divinity without me to count the nuts," Mr. Freestone said. He cast off and rowed toward *Sea Treader*.

"I'll wait for you," the young man called.

"No you won't," Mr. Freestone called back. "You go keep your father-in-law happy so you can remain the big deal."

The young man shook his head. He glanced at me.

"Can he really sail that thing?"

"He can sail it," I said.

"I think he's flipped. I honestly think he's flipped." He started away. "Growing a moustache at his age." He watched Mr. Freestone hoist the jib. "They're going to fire him sure as hell. At sixty years old he's going to be without a job."

"Well you can support him."

I had no right to say it, and the young man looked hard at me. He was a dude in those purple clothes and clogs, but he wasn't soft. I would've hated to fight him.

He frowned, rubbed his nose, and walked to his Lincoln. He stood a while to watch Mr. Freestone set his sails and head toward the bay.

Mr. Freestone stayed out until dark. In the moonlight he shifted his gear to the skiff and rowed to the wharf. He sang. I helped him unload. He was drunk.

"Would you believe I once tried to be a songwriter?" he asked. "At least I wrote one song about a wife who remembers a boy who brought her roses and a husband who dreams of a girl he danced with on a summer terrace."

He had the pint in his hand and drank.

"I actually tried to get the song published. Can't even remember all the words now. Do you want to hear the first line?"

"Sure."

He raised his voice, a surprisingly strong baritone, and sang over the water:

> It's nobody's fault and it's everyone's
> That the veil of all dreams is torn.

He stopped singing and swayed.

"I was not without dreams," he said.

He drank.

"Really a terrible song, and I'm sorry I subjected you to it," he said. "You're a fine young stalwart with his dreams intact, and when you marry that pretty girl, E. B. Freestone will dance at your wedding."

I wanted to take him to his motel, but he wouldn't allow it. He collected his gear, walked unsteadily to his Buick, and drove off. I heard the shells crackling a long time after I could no longer see his red taillights.

Toward the end of October the hot days ended. Wind blew from the north. The cold turned the marsh grass pale yellow. Gulls and fish hawks had to work against the wind, which finally swept the sky bare. The sound of buoy bells jarred the night.

Then in November, days again became golden, the year's last splurge before giving up to winter. The restless water still had the heat of summer in it. Birds returned too—herons and cranes winging along the shore.

As soon as school was out in the afternoon, I'd carry my rod to the point and surf cast for drum. The big fish hit hard and pulled me into the waves. Laura Lee sat among dunes, her arms around her knees, her dark hair blowing in the gusts.

On a Friday morning when I didn't have classes because of a teachers' meeting, Mr. Freestone appeared at the landing. I hadn't seen him for a couple of weeks. He wore his blue blazer, white slacks, and white deck shoes. He had on his yachting cap with its insignia of crossed anchors.

"Is it all right if I wear the cap now?" he asked.

"It's all right," I said. I was glad to see him.

He had his hamper, but for the first time since he started bringing candy no Virginia Divinity. He gazed at *Sea Treader* and down the river toward the bay. He breathed deeply. The wind had shifted to the northwest. It rippled his gray sideburns.

I helped him with his gear. We loaded the skiff. He walked to the store to buy cigars from Mr. Peters. They came out onto the porch where they talked, laughed, and shook hands. Mr. Freestone went to his Buick. From it he brought a small package.

"I was going to throw this away," he said and handed me the package.

I tore off the brown wrapping paper. Inside was a book with a faded red cover. It was *Captain Blood*.

"You can thank me by rowing me out," he said.

I rowed him and handed his gear aboard. He pumped *Sea Treader*, raised her sails, and cast free. She fell off the wind. Her canvas snapped and filled.

Mr. Freestone stood by the tiller. He trimmed his sails. He was moving away fast, his wake fizzing. He called, waved, and sang. I could just hear his voice. He settled by the tiller, adjusted his cap, and held the pint up as if making a toast.

I rowed back to the wharf. I was helping Amos White tar his boat. The tar steamed and bubbled in an iron kettle. From time to time we glanced up to search for a flash of sail. Mr. Freestone tacked past the black buoy and moved out of eye.

By late afternoon he hadn't returned. Amos and I put away our swabs and went inside to have a sandwich and Sunrise with Mr. Peters. The last shadows crossed the water. The river and bay weren't rough, and the wind held steady, but at dark we walked down to the wharf to look.

"You see him?" Mr. Peters called from the porch. He clinked his keys.

"No."

At ten o'clock I lit a lantern and hung it on the end of the wharf. Mr. Freestone didn't really need the lantern because the moon was shiny on the water. Wind shredded gongs of the buoy bells.

Mr. Peters, Amos, and I waited in the store. Occasionally we walked to the porch to look for Mr. Freestone's running lights. Once we believed we saw them, but the lights belonged to a fishing boat chugging up the river.

We dozed through the night. In the morning the wind hadn't changed, but the moist air had turned cold. We asked watermen to watch for *Sea Treader*.

Mr. Peters and I went out in his powerboat.

"What was his heading?" he called to me from the wheel. I was at the bow.

"South by east."

"Toward the ocean."

"That's right."

We went in at noon and notified the Coast Guard. A young lieutenant drove to the landing in a jeep. Wind ruffled blond hair on his neck. He filled out a report.

"We'll make some flights," he said.